SATAN IN THE SUBURBS
AND OTHER STORIES

# SATAN
## IN THE SUBURBS
### AND OTHER STORIES

*by*
BERTRAND RUSSELL

*illustrated by*
ÀSGEIR SCOTT

SPOKESMAN

First published in 1953 by *The Bodley Head*
This edition published in 2000 by
Spokesman
Russell House
Bulwell Lane, Nottingham NG6 0BT, England
Phone 0115 9708318.
Fax 0115 9420433.
e-mail elfeurocompuserve.com
www.spokesmanbooks.com
©Bertrand Russell Peace Foundation 2000

All rights reserved. No part of this publication may be reproduced, stored in a retrieval system or transmitted in any form or by any means electronic, mechanical, photocopying, recording or otherwise, without the prior permission of the publishers.

ISBN 0 85124 628 1 *paper*

A CIP Catalogue record is available from the British Library.

Printed by Russell Press Ltd (phone 0115 9784505)

CONTENTS

*Preface—page 7*

*Satan in the Suburbs or Horrors Manufactured Here—page 9*

*The Corsican Ordeal of Miss X—page 61*

*The Infra-redioscope—page 85*

*The Guardians of Parnassus—page 112*

*Benefit of Clergy—page 124*

PREFACE

To attempt a new departure at the age of eighty is perhaps unusual, though not unprecedented: Hobbes was older when he wrote his autobiography in Latin hexameters. Nevertheless, a few words may be in order, to mitigate any surprise that might be felt. I do not think that the reader's surprise to find me attempting stories can be greater than my own. For some reason entirely unknown to me I suddenly wished to write the stories in this volume, although I had never before thought of doing such a thing. I am incapable of critical judgement in this field, and I do not know whether the stories have any value. All that I know is that it gave me pleasure to write them and that therefore there may be people who will find pleasure in reading them.

The stories are not intended to be realistic—I am afraid disappointment awaits any reader who is led to search for Ghibelline castles in Corsica or diabolical philosophers in Mortlake. Nor have they any other serious purpose. The one which I wrote first, 'The Corsican Ordeal of Miss X,' attempted to combine the moods of 'Zuleika Dobson' and 'The Mysteries of Udolpho,' but the others, so far as I am aware, have less relation to previous models. I should be very sorry if it were supposed that the stories are meant to point a moral or illustrate a doctrine. Each of them was written for its own sake, simply as a story, and if it is found either interesting or amusing it has served its purpose.

'The Corsican Ordeal of Miss X' was published anonymously in the Christmas number of 'GO', 1951,

## SATAN IN THE SUBURBS or
## HORRORS MANUFACTURED HERE

### I

I live in Mortlake, and take the train daily to my work. On returning one evening I found a new brass plate on the gate of a villa which I pass every day. To my surprise, the brass plate, instead of making the usual medical announcement, said:

HORRORS MANUFACTURED HERE
Apply Dr. Murdoch Mallako

This announcement intrigued me, and when I got home I wrote a letter asking for further information, to enable me to decide whether or not to become a client of Dr. Mallako. I received the following reply:

Dear Sir,
    It is not wholly surprising that you should desire a few words of explanation concerning my brass plate. You may have observed

a recent tendency to deplore the humdrum uniformity of life in the suburbs of our great metropolis. The feeling has been expressed by some, whose opinion should carry weight, that adventure, and even a spice of danger, would make life more bearable for the victim of uniformity.

It is in the hope of supplying this need that I have embarked upon a wholly novel profession. I believe that I can supply my clients with new thrills and excitements such as will completely transform their lives.

If you wish for further information it will be given if you make an appointment. My charges are ten guineas an hour.

This reply made me suppose that Dr. Mallako was a philanthropist of a new species, and I debated with myself whether I should seek further information at the cost of ten guineas, or should keep this sum to be spent on some other pleasure.

Before I had resolved this question in my own mind I happened, on passing his gate one Monday evening, to observe my neighbour Mr. Abercrombie, emerging from the doctor's front door, pale and distraught, with wandering, unfocused eyes and tottering steps, fumbling at the latch of the gate and emerging on to the street, as though he were lost in some entirely strange locality.

'For God's sake, man,' I exclaimed, 'what has been happening to you?'

'Oh, nothing particular,' Mr. Abercrombie replied, with a pathetic attempt at an appearance of calm, 'we were talking about the weather.'

'Do not attempt to deceive me,' I replied, 'something even worse than the weather has stamped that horror upon your features.'

'Horror? Nonsense!' he replied testily, 'his whisky is very potent.'

Since he evidently wished to be rid of my inquiries I left him to find his own way home, and for some days I heard no more of him. Next evening I was returning at the same hour when I saw another neighbour, Mr. Beauchamp, emerging in the same condition of dazed terror, but when I accosted him, he waved me off. The next day I witnessed the same spectacle in the person of

Mr. Cartwright. On the Thursday evening Mrs. Ellerker, a married lady of forty, with whom I had been on friendly terms, rushed from his door and fainted on the pavement. I supported her while she revived, but when she recovered she uttered only one word, whispered shudderingly; the one word was 'never.' Nothing further was to be got from her, although I accompanied her to the door of her house.

On the Friday I saw nothing, and on Saturday and Sunday I did not go to work, and therefore did not pass Dr. Mallako's gate. But on Sunday evening my neighbour, Mr. Gosling, a substantial city man, dropped in for a chat. After I had supplied him with a drink and settled him in my most comfortable chair, he began, as was his wont, to gossip about our local acquaintance.

'Have you heard,' said he, 'what odd things are happening in our street? Mr. Abercrombie, Mr. Beauchamp, and Mr. Cartwright have all been taken ill and have stayed away from their respective offices, while Mrs. Ellerker lies in a dark room, moaning.'

Mr. Gosling evidently knew nothing about Dr. Mallako and his strange brass plate, so I decided to say nothing to him but to investigate on my own account. I visited in turn Mr. Abercrombie, Mr. Beauchamp, and Mr. Cartwright, but all of them refused to utter a single word. Mrs. Ellerker remained invisible in her invalid seclusion. It seemed clear that something very strange was happening and that Dr. Mallako was at the bottom of it. I decided to call upon him, not as a client, but as an investigator. I rang his bell and was shown by a trim parlour-maid into his well-appointed consulting room.

'And what, Sir, can I do for you?' he asked as he entered, smiling. His manners were suave, but his smile was enigmatic. His glance was penetrating and cold; and when his mouth smiled, his eyes did not. Something about his eyes caused me inexplicably to shudder.

'Dr. Mallako,' I said, 'accident causes me to pass your gate every evening, except Saturdays and Sundays, and on four successive evenings I have witnessed strange phenomena, all of which had a common character which I find not unalarming. I do not know, in view of your somewhat enigmatic letter, what lies behind the announcement of your brass plate, but the little that I have seen has caused me to doubt whether your purpose is as purely philanthropic as you led me to suppose. It may be that I am mistaken in this, and if so, it should be easy for you to set my mind at rest. But I confess that I shall not be satisfied until you have given me some explanation of the strange condition in which Mr. Abercrombie, Mr. Beauchamp, Mr. Cartwright, and Mrs. Ellerker emerged from your consulting-room.'

As I was speaking, the smile disappeared, and Dr. Mallako assumed a severe and reprehending demeanour.

'Sir,' he said, 'you are inviting me to commit an infamy. Do you not know that clients' confidences to a doctor are as inviolate as the confessional? Are you not aware that if I were to gratify your idle curiosity I should be guilty of a nefarious action? Have you lived so long without learning that a doctor's discretion must be observed? No, Sir, I shall not answer your impertinent queries, and I must request you to leave my house at once. There's the door.'

When I found myself again in the street I felt for a moment somewhat abashed. If he were indeed an orthodox medical practitioner, his answer to my inquiries would have been wholly correct. Could it be that I had been mistaken? Was it possible that he had disclosed to all four of his clients some painful medical misfortune of which until that moment they had been ignorant? It might indeed be so. It seemed improbable, but what further could I do?

I watched for another week, during which I again passed his gate every morning and evening, but I saw nothing further. I found, however, that I could not forget the strange doctor. Night after night he would appear before me in nightmares, sometimes with hooves and tail and with his brass plate worn as a breast-plate, sometimes with eyes glaring out of the darkness, and almost invisible lips forming the words 'YOU WILL COME!' Each day I passed his gate more slowly than on the previous day. Each day I felt a more powerful impulse to enter, this time not as an investigator, but as a client. Although I recognized the impulse as an insane obsession, I could not get rid of it. The horrid attraction gradually destroyed my work. At last I visited my chief, and without mentioning Dr. Mallako, persuaded him that I was suffering from over-work and needed a holiday. My chief, a much older man, for whom I entertained a profound respect, after one glance at my haggard features, granted my request with kindly solicitude.

I flew to Corfu, hoping that sun and sea would enable me to forget. But alas, no rest came to me there, by day or by night. Each night the eyes, even larger than before, glared at me while I dreamt. Each night I would wake in a cold sweat, hearing the ghostly voice saying 'COME!' At last I decided that if there were a cure for my condition it was not to be found in a holiday, and in despair I returned, hoping that the scientific research upon which I was engaged, and in which I had been passionately interested, would restore to me a measure of sanity. I plunged feverishly into a very abstruse scientific investigation, and I found a way to and from the station which did not pass Dr. Mallako's gate.

II

I began to think that perhaps the obsession was fading, when one evening Mr. Gosling again visited me. He was cheerful, rubicund, and rotund—just the man, I thought, to dispel such morbid fancies as had robbed me of my peace of mind. But his very first words, after I had supplied him with liquid refreshment, plunged me again into the lowest depths of terror.

'Have you heard,' said he, 'that Mr. Abercrombie has been arrested?'

'Good God!' I exclaimed, 'Mr. Abercrombie arrested? What can he have done?'

'Mr. Abercrombie, as you know,' Mr. Gosling replied, 'has been a respectable and respected manager of a very important branch of one of our leading banks. His life, both professional and private, has been always blameless, as was his father's before him. It was confidently expected that in the next Birthday Honours List he would receive a knighthood, and a movement was on foot to have him chosen as Parliamentary candidate for the Division. But in spite of this long and honourable record, it appears that he has suddenly stolen a large sum of money, and has made a dastardly attempt to place the blame upon a subordinate.'

Having hitherto regarded Mr. Abercrombie as a friend, I was deeply distressed by this news. As yet, he was on remand, and after some difficulty I persuaded the prison authorities to allow me to visit him. I found him emaciated and haggard, listless and despairing. At first he stared at me as though I were a stranger, and he only gradually became aware that he was seeing a former friend. I could not but connect his present disastrous condition with his visit to Dr. Mallako, and I felt that perhaps, if I could pierce the mystery, I should find some explanation of his sudden guilt.

'Mr. Abercrombie,' I said, 'you will remember that on a former occasion I tried to discover the cause of your strange behaviour, but you refused to reveal anything. For God's sake, do not again rebuff me. You see what has come of your previous reserve. Tell me the truth, I beseech you, for it may be not yet too late.'

'Alas!' he replied, 'the time for your well-meant efforts is past. For me there remains only a wearisome waiting for death—for my poor wife and my unhappy children, penury and shame. Unhappy moment in which I passed that accursed gate! Unhappy house in which I listened to the devilish insight of that malignant fiend!'

'I feared as much,' said I, 'but tell me all.'

'I visited Dr. Mallako,' so Mr. Abercrombie began his confession, 'in a spirit of carefree curiosity. What sort of horrors, I wondered, did Dr. Mallako manufacture? What hope could he entertain of making a living out of persons who enjoyed his romances? There could not, I thought, be many like myself, willing to spend money in so idle a fashion. Dr. Mallako, however, appeared completely self-assured. He treated me, not as most of the inhabitants of Mortlake, even the most substantial ones, were in the habit of treating me, as an important citizen whom it would be wise to conciliate. On the contrary, he treated me from the first with a kind of superiority which had in it a touch of disdain. And from his first sharp scrutiny I felt that he could read even my most secret thoughts.

'At first this seemed to me no more than a foolish fancy, and I tried to shake it off, but as his talk proceeded in even tones at an unchanging pace, and without the faintest indication of feeling, I fell gradually more and more under the spell. My will abandoned me, and strange secret thoughts which until that moment had not entered my consciousness except in nightmares came to the surface, like monsters of the deep emerging from their dark caves to bring horror to the crews of whalers. Like a derelict ship in the waste places of the Southern Seas, I drifted upon the tempest of his own creating, helpless, hopeless, but fascinated.'

'But what,' I interrupted, 'was Dr. Mallako saying to you all this time? I cannot help you if your language is so vague and metaphorical. Concrete details are what I must have if Counsel is to be of any use to you.'

He sighed deeply, and proceeded: 'At first we conversed in a desultory manner about this and that. I mentioned friends of mine whom harsh business conditions had ruined. Under the influence of his apparent sympathy I confessed that I also had reason to fear ruin. "Ah, well," he said, "there is always a way to avert ruin if one is willing to take it.

' "I have a friend whose circumstances at one time were not very different from yours at the present moment. He also was a bank manager; he also was trusted; he also speculated and faced ruin. But he was not the man to sit down tamely under such a prospect. He realized that he had certain assets: his apparently blameless life, his satisfactory performance of all the tasks imposed by his professional duties, and, what perhaps was not the least of these assets, a man immediately beneath him in the hierarchy of the bank who had allowed himself to acquire the repute of being somewhat harum-scarum, not quite so correct in behaviour as becomes a man entrusted to deal with other people's money, not always sedate, sometimes the worse for liquor, and at least once in this condition guilty of uttering subversive political opinions.

' "My friend," so Dr. Mallako continued, after a short pause, during which he sipped his whisky, "my friend realized, and this perhaps is the best proof of his ability, that should any defalcations be discovered in the bank's accounts, it would not be difficult to throw suspicion upon this irresponsible young man. My friend prepared the ground very carefully. Without the young man's knowledge, he hid in the young man's flat a bundle of bank notes abstracted from the bank. Over the telephone, nominally in the young man's name, he placed large bets on horses which did not win a place. He reckoned correctly the number of days which would elapse before the bookmaker wrote indignant letters to the young man complaining of non-payment. At exactly the right moment he allowed it to be discovered that there was a huge loss in the bank's cash. He communicated at once with the police, and, apparently distraught, he reluctantly allowed the police to drag from him the name of the young man as the only possible suspect. The police proceeded to the young man's flat, found the bundle of notes and read with considerable interest the indignant communication from the bookmaker. Needless to say, the young man was sent to prison, and the manager was more trusted than ever. His speculations on the Stock Exchange from this moment onwards were more cautious than they had been. He made a large fortune, became a baronet, and was chosen to represent his constituency in Parliament. But of his ultimate activities as a Cabinet Minister it would be indiscreet of me to speak. From this true story," said Dr. Mallako, "you will see that a little enterprise and a little ingenuity can turn threatened defeat into triumph, and secure the profound respect of all right-minded citizens." '

'While he spoke,' Mr. Abercrombie resumed, 'my mind was in a turmoil. I myself was in difficulties through rash speculations. I myself had a subordinate who had all the characteristics of the young man denounced by Dr. Mallako's friend. I myself, though my thoughts had hardly aspired so high as to a baronetcy, had toyed with the hope of a knighthood and a seat in Parliament. These hopes would have a firm foundation if my present difficulties could be surmounted; if not, I was faced by the prospect of poverty, perhaps disgrace. I thought of my wife, who shared my hopes, and had visions of herself as Lady Abercrombie, compelled perhaps to keep a seaside boarding house, and not (so I feared) slow to point out to me morning, noon and night, the afflictions which my folly had brought upon her head. I thought of my two sons, now both at a good public school, looking forward to an honourable career, in which athletic honours should pave the way for responsible posts. I thought of these sons, suddenly taken away from their paradise, compelled to attend some plebeian secondary school, and at the age of eighteen to adopt some obscure and humdrum means of livelihood. I thought of my neighbours in Mortlake, no longer genial, but passing me in the street with averted looks, unwilling to share a drink or listen to my opinions on the Chinese imbroglio.

'All these visions of horror floated through my mind as Dr. Mallako's calm and even voice inexorably proceeded. "How can I endure all this?" I thought. "Never, while any way of escape presents itself. But can I, I who am no longer young, I whose career has hitherto been blameless, I whom all my neighbours greet with a smile, can I suddenly abandon all this security for the dangerous existence of a criminal?" Could I live, day after day and night after night, with the dread of discovery hanging over me? Could I preserve before my wife that air of calm superiority upon which my domestic bliss depended? Could I continue as heretofore to greet my sons on their return from school with the moral maxims that are expected of a substantial parent? Could I inveigh with conviction in my railway carriage about the inefficiency of the police and their lamentable failure to catch criminals whose depredations were shaking the pillars of the financial order? I realized with a cold shudder of doubt that if I should fail in any of these things after acting like Dr. Mallako's friend, I should be liable to incur suspicion. There would be those who would say: "I wonder what has happened to Mr. Abercrombie. He used to utter his sentiments with full-blooded gusto in a loud and convincing tone, such as would cause any malefactor to quake, but now, though the same sentiments come from his lips, he whispers and stutters while he utters them, and I have even seen him looking over his shoulder when speaking of the inefficiency of the police. I find this puzzling, and I cannot but think that there is some mystery about Mr. Abercrombie."

'This painful vision grew more and more vivid in my tortured imagination. I saw in my mind's eye my neighbours in Mortlake and my friends in the City comparing notes and at last arriving at the grim conclusion that the change in my manner closely synchronized with the famous disaster at my bank. From this discovery, I feared it would be but a step to my downfall. "No," I thought, "never will I listen to the voice of this sinister tempter. Never will I abandon the path of duty!" And yet . . . and yet. . . .

'How easy it all seemed, as the soothing voice went on and on, with its suave history of triumph. And had I not read somewhere that the trouble with our world is unwillingness to take risks? Had not some eminent philosopher enunciated the maxim that one should live dangerously? Was it not perhaps even in some higher sense my duty to listen to such teaching, and put it into practice with such means as circumstances placed at my disposal? Contending arguments, contending hopes and fears, contending habits and aspirations produced in me an utterly bewildering turmoil. At last I could bear it no longer. "Dr. Mallako," I exclaimed, "I do not know whether you are an angel or a devil, but I do know that I would to God I had never met you." It was at this point that I rushed from the house and met you at the gate.

'Never since that fatal interview have I enjoyed a moment's peace of mind. By day I looked at all whom I met and thought to myself: "What would they do if . . .?" At night before I slept alternate horrors of ruin and prison buffeted me this way and that in an endless game of battledore and shuttlecock. My wife complained of my restlessness, and at last insisted upon my sleeping in my dressing-room. There, when tardy sleep came, it was more terrible even than the hours of wakefulness. In nightmares I walked along a narrow alley between a workhouse and a prison. I was seized with fever, and tottered this way and that across the street, constantly falling almost into one or other of these dreadful buildings. I would see a policeman advancing upon me, and as his hand fell upon my shoulder, I would awake, shrieking.

'It is not to be wondered at if, in these circumstances, my affairs became more and more involved. My speculations grew wilder, and my debts mounted up. At last it seemed to me that no hope remained unless I copied Dr. Mallako's friend. But in my distraught state I made mistakes which he did not make. The notes which I planted in the apartment of my harum-scarum subordinate bore my finger-prints. The telephone message to the bookmaker was proved by the police to have come from my house. The horse which I had confidently expected to lose, won the race to the surprise of everyone. This made the police the more ready to believe my subordinate when he denied ever having placed such a bet. All the hopeless entanglement of my affairs was laid bare by Scotland Yard. My subordinate, whom I had supposed to be a man of no account, turned out to be the nephew of a Cabinet Minister.

'None of this bad luck, I am sure, caused any surprise to Dr. Mallako. He, I do not doubt, foresaw from the very first the whole course of events up to the present frightful moment. For me nothing remains but to take my punishment. Dr. Mallako, I fear, has committed no legal crime, but oh, if you can find some method of bringing upon his head one-tenth of the sorrow that he has brought upon mine, you will know that in one of Her Majesty's prisons, one grateful heart is thanking you!'

Wrung with compassion, I bade farewell to Mr. Abercrombie, promising to bear his last words in mind.

III

Mr. Abercrombie's last words greatly increased the already intense horror which I felt towards Dr. Mallako, but to my bewilderment I found that this increase of horror was accompanied by an increase of fascination. I could not forget the terrible doctor. I wished him to suffer, but I wished him to suffer through me, and I wished that at least once there should be between him and me some passage as deep and dark and terrible as the things that looked out of his eyes. I found, however, no way of gratifying either of these contradictory wishes, and for some time I continued the endeavour to become wholly absorbed in my scientific researches. I had begun to have some degree of success in this endeavour when I was plunged once more into the world of horror from which I had been trying to emerge. This happened through the misfortunes of Mr. Beauchamp.

Mr. Beauchamp, a man of about thirty-five years of age, had been known to me for a number of years as a pillar of virtue in Mortlake. He was secretary of a society concerned in distributing Bibles, and he was also concerned in purity work. He wore always a very old and shiny black coat and striped trousers which had seen better days. His tie was black, his manner earnest. Even in the train he was liable to quote texts. Every species of alcoholic drink he spoke of as 'fermented liquor,' and not the faintest sip ever passed his lips. When he spilt a cup of scalding coffee all over himself, he exclaimed: 'Dear me, how very annoying!' In a society of men only, if he was sufficiently assured of the earnestness of his companions, he would sometimes regret the sad frequency of what he called 'carnal intercourse.' Late dinners were an abomination to him; he always had a high tea, which before the war used to consist

of cold meat, pickles, and a boiled potato, but in the days of austerity omitted the cold meat. His hand was always moist, and his handshake limp. There was not one person in Mortlake who could recall one single action of his for which even he would have had cause to blush.

But shortly before the time when I had seen him emerging from Dr. Mallako's gate, something of a change had been observed in his demeanour. The black coat and striped trousers gave way to a dark grey suit with trousers of the same material. The black tie was replaced by a dark blue tie. His allusions to the Bible became less frequent, and he could, of an evening, see men drinking without being led into a discourse on the virtue of temperance. Once, and once only, he was seen hurrying along the street towards the station wearing a red carnation in his buttonhole. This indiscretion, which set all Mortlake agog, was not repeated. But the gossips were provided with fresh material by an event which occurred a few days after the red carnation. Mr. Beauchamp was seen in a very smart motor-car, sitting beside a young and lovely lady, whose dressmaker was obviously Parisian. For a few days everybody asked the question: 'Who can she be?' Mr. Gosling, as usual, was the first to supply the gossip demanded. I, like others, had been intrigued by the change in Mr. Beauchamp, and one evening when Mr. Gosling came to see me, he said:

'Have you heard who the lady is who is having so marked an effect upon our holy neighbour?'

'No,' I replied.

'Well,' he said, 'I have just ascertained who she is. She is Yolande Molyneux, widow of Captain Molyneux, whose painful end in the jungles of Burma during the last war was one of the innumerable tragedies of that time. The lovely Yolande, however, overcame her grief without much difficulty. Captain Molyneux, as you of course remember, was the only son of the famous soap manufacturer, and as his father's heir, he was already possessed of an ample fortune, doubtless with a view to minimizing death duties. This ample fortune has come to his widow, who is a lady of insatiable curiosity about various types of men. She has known millionaires and mountebanks, Montenegrin mountaineers and Indian fakirs. She is catholic in her tastes, but prefers whatever is bizarre. In her wanderings over the surface of our planet she had not previously made the acquaintance of Low Church sanctimony, and meeting it in the person of Mr. Beauchamp, she found it a fascinating study. I shudder to think what she will make of poor Mr. Beauchamp, for while he is in deadly earnest, she is merely adding a new specimen to her collection.'

I felt that this boded ill for Mr. Beauchamp, but I failed to foresee the depth of disaster that lay ahead of him, since I did not at that time know of the activities of Dr. Mallako. It was only after I had heard Mr. Abercrombie's story that I realized what Dr. Mallako might make of such material. Since he himself was unapproachable, I managed to make the acquaintance of the lovely Yolande, who lived in a fine old house on Ham Common. I found, however, to my disappointment that she knew nothing of Dr. Mallako, whom Mr. Beauchamp had never mentioned to her. She spoke of Mr. Beauchamp always with amused and contemptuous toleration, and regretted his efforts to adapt himself to what he supposed to be her tastes.

'I like his texts,' she said, 'and I used to like his striped trousers. I like his stern refusal to partake of "fermented liquor," and I enjoy his stern repudiation of even such mild words as "blast" and "blow." It is these things that make him interesting to me, and the more he endeavours to resemble a normal human being, the more difficult I find it to preserve with him a friendly demeanour, without which his passion would drive him to despair. It is useless, however, to attempt to explain this to the dear man, since the whole matter is beyond his psychological comprehension.'

I found it useless to appeal to Mrs. Molyneux to spare the poor man.

'Nonsense,' she would say, 'a little glimpse of feelings outside the domain of sanctimony will do him good. He will emerge more able to deal with the sinners who occupy the focus of his interests than he has hitherto been. I consider myself a philanthropist, and almost a participant in his work. You will see, before I have done with him, his power of rescuing sinners will be augmented a hundredfold. Every twinge of his own conscience will be transformed into burning rhetoric, and his hope that he himself may not be irretrievably damned will enable him to offer the prospect of ultimate salvation even to those whom he has hitherto regarded as utterly degraded. But enough of Mr. Beauchamp,' she continued with a light laugh, 'I am sure that after this dry conversation you will wish to wash away the taste of Mr. Beauchamp by one of my very special cocktails.'

Such conversations with Mrs. Molyneux were, I saw, completely futile, and Dr. Mallako remained aloof and unapproachable. Mr. Beauchamp himself, when I tried to see him, was invariably setting off towards Ham Common, if he was not busy with the affairs of his office. It was observed, however, that these affairs occupied him less and less, and that the evening train in which he had been accustomed to return no longer found him in his usual place. Although I continued to hope for the best, I feared the worst.

It was my fears that proved justified. One evening, as I was passing his house, I observed a crowd at his door, and his elderly housekeeper in tears, beseeching them to go away. I knew the good lady, having often visited Mr. Beauchamp, and I therefore asked her what was the matter.

'My poor master,' she said, 'Oh, my poor master!'

'What has happened to your poor master?' I asked.

'Oh, Sir, never shall I forget the dreadful sight that met my eyes when I opened the door of his study. His study, as you might know, was used long ago as a larder, and there are still hooks in the ceiling from which, in more spacious days, hams and legs of mutton used to be suspended. From one of these hooks, as I opened the door, I saw poor Mr. Beauchamp hanging by a rope. An overturned chair lay on its side just beneath the poor gentleman, and I am forced to suppose that some sorrow had driven him to the rash act. What this sorrow may have been I do not know, but I darkly suspect the wicked woman whose wiles have been leading him astray!'

Nothing further was to be learned from her, but I thought it possible that her suspicions might be not unfounded, and that the perfidious Yolande might be able to throw some light upon the tragedy. I went immediately to her house, and found her in the very act of reading a letter which had just arrived by special messenger.

'Mrs. Molyneux,' I said, 'our relations hitherto have been merely social, but the time has come for graver speech. Mr. Beauchamp has been my friend; he has hoped to be something more than a friend to you. It is possible that you may be able to throw some light upon the dreadful event which has occurred in his house.'

'It *is* possible,' she said, with something rather more than her wonted seriousness. 'I have this very moment finished reading the last words of that unhappy man, the depth of whose feelings I now know that I misjudged. I will not deny that I have been to blame, but it is not I who am the chief culprit. That role belongs to an individual more sinister and more serious than myself. I allude to Dr. Mallako. His part is revealed in the letter which I have been reading. Since you were a friend of Mr. Beauchamp, and as I know that you are the sworn enemy of Dr. Mallako, I think it only right that you should see this letter.'

With these words she put it into my hands, and I took my leave. I could not bring myself to read the letter until I was in my own house, and even then it was with trembling fingers that I unfolded its many sheets. The evil aura of the strange doctor seemed to envelop me as I spread them on my knees. And it was with the utmost difficulty that I prevented myself from being blinded by the vision of his baleful eyes, which made it almost impossible to read the terrible words which it was my duty to study. At last, however, I pulled myself together, and forced myself to become immersed in the torments which had driven poor Mr. Beauchamp to his desperate act. Mr. Beauchamp's letter was as follows:

My very dear Yolande,
    I do not know whether the contents of this letter will come to you as a sorrow or as a relief from embarrassment. However that may be, I feel that my last words on earth must be addressed to you—for these are my last words. When I have finished this letter, I shall be no more.

My life, as you know, was drab and colourless until you came into it. Since I have known you, I have become aware that there are things of value in human existence in addition to prohibitions and the dusty 'don'ts' to which my activities have been devoted. Although all has ended in disaster, I cannot even now bring myself to regret the sweet moments in which you have seemed to smile upon me. But it is not of feelings that I am now to write.

Never until now, in spite of your not unnatural curiosity, have I revealed to you what it was that occurred when, shortly after I had made your acquaintance, I paid a fateful visit to Dr. Mallako. At the time of that visit I had begun to wish that I were the kind of dashing figure that might impress your dear imagination, and had begun to look upon my past self as that of a dismal sanctimonious dolt. A new life, I felt, would be possible for me if I could but win your esteem. I did not, however, see any way in which this could be possible until my ill-omened visit to that malignant incarnation of Satan.

On the afternoon upon which I called upon him, he received me with a genial smile, took me to his consulting-room, and said:

'Mr. Beauchamp, it is a great pleasure to see you here. I have heard much of your good works, and have admired your devotion to noble causes. It is, I must confess, somewhat difficult for me to conceive any way in which I can be of use to you, but if such a way exists, you have only to command me. Before we proceed to business, however, a little refreshment might be not amiss. I am well aware that you do not partake of the juice of the grape, or the distilled essence of grain, and I would not insult you by offering either, but perhaps a nice cup of cocoa, adequately sweetened, would be not unwelcome.'

I thanked him, not only for his kindness, but for his knowledge of my tastes, and after his housekeeper had supplied the cocoa, our serious colloquy began. Some magnetic quality in him elicited from me a degree of unreserve which I had not anticipated. I told him about you; I told him my hopes and I told him my fears; I told him the change in my aspirations and beliefs; I told him the intoxicating moments of kindness, which enabled me to live through the long days when you were cold; I told him how conscious I was that if I were to win you I must have more to offer, more in worldly goods, but not in worldly goods only—more also in richness of character and conversational variety. If he could help me to achieve all this, I said, he would put me forever in his debt, and the paltry ten guineas which I was to pay for the consultation would prove the best investment ever made by mortal man.

Dr. Mallako, after a moment's scrutiny, remarked in a meditative voice:

'Well, I am not certain whether what I am about to say will be of any use to you or not. But however that may be, I will tell you a little story which has a certain affinity with your case.

'I have a friend, a well-known man, whom perhaps you may have met in the course of your professional work, whose early years were spent much as yours have been. He, like you, fell in love with a charming lady. He early realized that he would have little hope of winning her unless he could acquire more wealth than his previous course of life was likely to bring him. He, like you, distributed Bibles in many languages and in many lands. One day in the train he met a publisher of a somewhat dubious reputation. At an earlier time he would not have spoken to such a man, but now the liberalizing influence of his amatory hopes made him more hospitable to types that he had hitherto considered without the pale.

'The publisher explained the immense international network by which dubious literature is got into the hands of those degenerates whom such pernicious stuff attracts. "The only difficulty," said the publisher, "lies in advertising. There is no difficulty about secret distribution, but secret advertising is almost a contradiction in terms." At this point the publisher's eyes twinkled and, with a mischievous smile, he said: "Now if we had someone like you to help us, the whole problem of advertising would be solved. You could, in the Bibles that you distribute, have occasional pointers. For example, when we are told that the heart is desperately wicked and deceitful above all things (Jeremiah xvii. 9), you will put a footnote saying that further information about the wickedness of the human heart can be obtained from Messrs. So & So on application. And when Judah tells his servants to look for the whore that is without the city gates, you will put a footnote saying that doubtless most readers of the Holy Book do not know the meaning of this word, but that Messrs. So & So will explain it on demand. And when the Word of God mentions the regrettable behaviour of Onan, another reference to us will be in order." The publisher, however, seemed to think that this was not the sort of thing that my friend would care to do, although of course, as he explained in a meditative and slightly regretful tone, if it were done, the profits would be colossal.

'My friend,' so Dr. Mallako continued, 'took very little time to come to a decision. When he and the publisher arrived at their London terminus, they adjourned to the publisher's club, and after a few drinks, concluded the main heads of their agreement. My friend continued to distribute Bibles, the Bibles were more in demand than ever, the publisher's profits rose, and my friend became rich enough to have a fine house and a fine car. He gradually ceased to quote the Bible, except those passages to which he had appended footnotes. His conversation became lively and his cynicism amusing. The lady, who had at first merely toyed with him, became fascinated. They married, and lived happy ever after. You may or may not find this story interesting, but I fear that it is the only contribution I can make to the solution of your perplexities.'

I was horrified by what I felt to be the wickedness of Dr. Mallako's suggestion. I felt it unthinkable that I, whose life had been governed hitherto by the straitest rules of rectitudes, should become associated with anything so universally execrated as the sale of obscene literature. I put this to Dr. Mallako in no uncertain terms. Dr. Mallako only smiled a wise and enigmatic smile.

'My friend,' said he, 'have you not been learning, ever since you had the good fortune to become acquainted with Mrs. Molyneux, that there is a certain narrowness in the code of behaviour that you have hitherto followed? You must, I am sure, at some period have read the Song of Solomon, and I feel convinced that you have wondered how it came to be included in the Word of God. Such wondering is impious. And if some of the literature distributed by my friend's publisher is not wholly unlike the work of the wise but uxorious king, it is illiberal, on that account, to find fault with it. A little freedom, a little daylight, a little fresh air, even on the subjects from which you have sought to avert your thoughts (vainly, I am afraid), can do nothing but good, and is indeed to be commended by the example of the Holy Book.'

'But is there not,' I said, 'a grave danger that the perusal of such literature may lead young men, ay, and young women too, into deadly sin? Can I look my fellow men in the face when I reflect that perhaps at this very moment some unwedded couple is enjoying unholy bliss as a result of acts from which I derive a pecuniary profit?'

'Alas,' Dr. Mallako replied, 'there is, I fear, much in our holy religion that you have failed adequately to understand. Have you reflected upon the parable of the ninety-nine just men who needed no repentance, and caused less joy in Heaven than the one sinner who returned to the fold? Have you never studied the text about the Pharisee and the Publican? Have you not allowed yourself to extract the moral from the penitent thief? Have you never asked yourself what it was that was blameworthy in the Pharisees whom our Lord denounced while eating their lunch? Have you never wondered at the praise of a broken and contrite heart? Can you say honestly that your heart, before you met Mrs. Molyneux, was either broken or contrite? Has it ever occurred to you that one cannot be contrite without first sinning? Yet this is the plain teaching of the Gospels. And if you wish to lead men into the frame of mind which is pleasing to God they must first sin. Doubtless many of those who buy the literature that my friend's publisher distributes will afterwards repent, and if we are to believe the teachings of our holy religion, they will then be more pleasing to their Maker than the impeccably righteous, among whom hitherto you have been a notable example.'

This logic confounded me, and I became perplexed in the extreme. But there remained one hesitation.

'Is there not,' I said, 'in such behaviour a terrible risk of detection? Is there not a very considerable likelihood that the police will discover the nefarious traffic from which these great profits are derived? Do not the prison gates yawn for the men who have been drawn into this illicit traffic?'

'Aha!' said Dr. Mallako, 'There are convolutions and ramifications in our social system that have remained unknown to you and your coadjutors. Do you suppose that where such large sums are involved there is no one among the authorities who, for a percentage, would be willing to co-operate, or, at least, shut his eyes? Such men, I can assure you, exist, and it is by their co-operation that my friend's publisher acquires security. If you should decide to copy his example, you have to make sure that official blindness is at your disposal.'

I could think of nothing more to say, and I left the house of Dr. Mallako in a state of doubt, not only as to what I should do, but as to the whole basis of morality, and the purpose of a good life.

At first doubt completely incapacitated me. I kept away from my office, and brooded darkly as to what I should do and how I should live. But gradually Dr. Mallako's arguments acquired a greater and greater hold over my imagination. 'I cannot resolve,' so I thought to myself, 'the ethical doubts which have been instilled into my mind. I do not know what conduct is right and what is wrong. But I do know (so I thought in my blindness) what is the road to the heart of my beloved Yolande.'

At last chance decided my final move, or at least I thought it was chance, though now I have my doubts. I met a man of exceptional worldly wisdom, a man who had wandered about the world in questionable activities and dubious localities. He professed to know the whole connection of the police with the underworld. He knew which policemen were incorruptible and which were not—so, at least, he said. It appeared that he made his living as an intermediary between would-be criminals and pliant policemen.

'But you, of course,' so he said, 'are not interested in such matters, seeing that your life is an open book, and that never, by a hair's breadth, have you been tempted to depart from legality.'

'That, of course, is true,' I replied, 'but at the same time I think it is my duty to enlarge my experience to the utmost, and if indeed you know any such policeman, I shall be glad if you will introduce me to him.'

He did so. He made me acquainted with Detective-Inspector Jenkins, who, so I was given to understand, had not that unbending virtue which most of us take for granted in our noble police force. I became gradually increasingly friendly with Inspector Jenkins, and by slow stages approached the subject of indecent publications, preserving always the guise of one solely concerned to acquire a knowledge of the world.

'I will introduce you,' he said, 'to a publisher of my acquaintance, one, I may say, with whom I have at various times done not unprofitable business.'

He duly introduced me to a Mr. Mutton, who, he said, was the sort of publisher that had been in question. I had not before heard of his firm, but that, after all, did not surprise me, as I was entering a wholly unfamiliar world. After some preliminary skirmishing, I suggested to Mr. Mutton that I could be useful to him in the way in which Dr. Mallako's friend had been useful to his publisher. Mr. Mutton did not reject the idea, but said that for his own protection he must have something from me in writing as to the nature of the proposal. Somewhat reluctantly I agreed.

All this happened only yesterday, while still bright hopes were leading me further and further towards perdition. Today—But how can I bring myself to reveal the dreadful truth, a truth which shows not only my wickedness, but also my incredible folly?—today a police constable presented himself at my front door. On being admitted, he showed me the document which I had signed at the request of Mr. Mutton.

'Is this your signature?' he said.

Although utterly astonished, I had the presence of mind to say:

'That is for you to prove.'

'Well,' said he, 'I do not think that will offer much difficulty, and you may as well know the situation in which you will then find yourself. Detective-Inspector Jenkins is not, as you had been led to suppose, a dishonest public servant. He is, on the contrary, a man devoted to the preservation of our national life from all taint of impurity, and the reputation of corruptibility which he has been careful to acquire exists only to draw criminals into his net. Mr. Mutton is a man of straw. Sometimes one detective, sometimes another, impersonates this nefarious character. You will perceive, Mr. Beauchamp, that your hopes of escape are slender.'

With that, he took his departure. I realized at once that no hope remained for me, and no possibility of an endurable life. Even should I be fortunate enough to escape prison, the document which I signed would put an end to the employment from which I have hitherto gained my livelihood. And the disgrace would make it impossible to face you, without whom, life can have no savour. Nothing remains for me but death. I go to meet my Maker, whose just wrath will, no doubt, condemn me to those torments which I have so often and so vividly depicted to others. But there is one sentence which I believe he will vouchsafe me before I depart from the Dread Presence. That one sentence shall be: 'Of all the wicked men that have ever lived, none can be more wicked, none more disastrously designing, than Dr. Mallako, whom, O Lord, I beseech Thee to reserve for some quite special depth in that hell where I am about to make my abode.'

This is all that I shall have to say to my Maker. To you, my fair one, out of the depths in which I am sunk, I wish all happiness and all joy.

IV

It was some time after the tragic fate of Mr. Beauchamp that I learned what had happened to Mr. Cartwright. I am happy to say that his fate was somewhat less dreadful, but it cannot be denied that it was not such as most people would welcome. I learned what had become of him partly from his own lips, partly from those of my only episcopal friend.

Mr. Cartwright, as everyone knows, was a famous artistic photographer, patronized by all the best film stars and politicians. He made a speciality of catching a characteristic expression, such as would induce all who saw the photograph to draw favourable inferences about the original. He had as his assistant a lady of extreme beauty, named Lalage Scraggs. Her beauty was marred for his clients only by a somewhat excessive langour. It was said, however, by those who knew them well, that towards Mr. Cartwright there was no such langour, but that the pair were united by an ardent passion, not, I regret to say, sanctified by any legal tie. Mr. Cartwright had, however, one great sorrow. Although he worked morning, noon, and night, with an impeccable artistic conscience, and although his clientele became more and more distinguished, he was unable, owing to the rapacious demands of the tax-gatherer, to gratify the somewhat expensive wishes of himself and the lovely Lalage.

'What is the good,' he was wont to say, 'of all this toil, when at least nine-tenths of my nominal earnings are seized by the Government to buy molybdenum or tungsten or some other substance in which I take no interest?'

The discontent thus engendered embittered his life, and he frequently contemplated retiring to the Principality of Monaco. When he saw Dr. Mallako's brass plate, he exclaimed:

'Can this worthy man have discovered any horror more horrifying than surtax? If so, he must indeed be a man of considerable imagination. I will consult him in the hope that he may enlarge my mind.'

Having secured an appointment, he visited Dr. Mallako on an afternoon when it so happened that he was not in demand for the photographing of any film star or Cabinet Minister or foreign diplomat. Even the Argentine Ambassador, who had promised to pay his fee in rounds of beef, had chosen a different date.

After the usual polite preliminaries, Dr. Mallako came to the point, and asked what type of horror Mr. Cartwright desired, 'for,' said Dr. Mallako, with a quiet smile, 'I have horrors to suit all customers.'

'Well,' said Mr. Cartwright, 'the horror I want is one concerned with methods of earning money that will escape the attention of the Tax Collector. I do not know whether you can invest this subject with such horror as your brass plate promises, but if you can, you will earn my gratitude.'

'I think,' said Dr. Mallako, 'that I can give you what you want. Indeed, my professional pride is involved, and I should be ashamed to fail you. I will tell you a little story which may perhaps help you to make up your mind.

'I have a friend who lives in Paris. He, like you, is a photographer of genius. He, like you, has a beautiful assistant who is not indifferent to Parisian pleasures. He, like you, found taxation irksome, so long as he confined himself to the legitimate exercise of his profession. He now still depends upon photography, but his methods are more progressive. He makes a practice of ascertaining at what hotel in Paris each of the stream of celebrities who visit that great city is to be expected. His beautiful assistant seats herself in the lobby at the time when the great man is about to arrive. While he is busy at the desk, she suddenly gasps, totters, and appears about to faint. The gallant gentleman, being the only male who enjoys sufficient proximity, inevitably rushes to her support. At the moment when she is in his arms, the camera clicks. Next day, my friend waits upon him with the developed photograph, and asks how much he will pay to have the negative and all the copies destroyed. If the victim is an eminent divine or an American politician, he is usually willing to pay a very considerable sum. By this means, my friend has improved upon the forty-hour week. His assistant works only one day in the week; he works on two days— the one when he first takes the photograph, and the other when he visits his victim. The remaining five days of each week the pair spend in bliss. Perhaps,' Dr. Mallako concluded, 'you may find something in this little story that may be of some use to you in your unfortunate perplexities.'

Only two things worried Mr. Cartwright about this suggestion. One was the fear of discovery, the other was a distaste for such apparently amatory promiscuity on the part of the fair Lalage. Fear conjured up visions of the police; jealousy, even more potent, suggested some possible celebrity whose arms Lalage might prefer to his own. But while he was still debating the matter in his mind, he received a demand for twelve thousands pounds for Income Tax and Surtax. Mr. Cartwright, to whom economy was wholly foreign, did not possess twelve thousand pounds in any available form, and after a few sleepless nights, he decided that there was nothing for it but to imitate Dr. Mallako's friend.

After suitable preparations and a survey of the field of possible celebrities, Mr. Cartwright decided that his first victim should be the Bishop of Boria-boola-ga, who was visiting London for a Pan-Anglican Congress. Everything went off like clockwork. The tottering lady fell into the arms of the Bishop, and the arms encircled her with no visible reluctance. Mr. Cartwright, concealed behind a screen, emerged at the right moment, and waited next day upon the Bishop with a very convincing photograph.

'This, my dear Bishop,' he said, 'is, as I am sure you will agree, an artistic masterpiece. I cannot but think that you will wish to possess it, since everyone knows of your passion for negro art, and this might well serve as a religious picture in some native cult. But in view of my overheads, and the large salary that I am compelled to pay to my highly skilled assistant, I cannot part with the negative and the few copies that I have made of it for less than a thousand pounds, and even this is a fee reduced to its lowest possible figure, out of sympathy for the well-known poverty of our Colonial Episcopate.'

'Well,' said the Bishop, 'this is a most unpleasant contretemps. You can hardly suppose that I possess a thousand pounds here and now. I will, however, since clearly you have me in your grip, give you an I.O.U. and a lien on the revenues of my See.'

Mr. Cartwright was much relieved to find the Bishop so reasonable, and they parted on almost friendly terms.

It so happened, however, that the Bishop in question differed in some important ways from the majority of his colleagues. He had been a friend of mine when I was at the university, and as an undergraduate he had been noted as a practical joker. Some of his jokes were perhaps not quite in the best of taste. People were surprised when he decided to take Orders, and still more surprised when they learned that, although his sermons were eloquent and convincing and although he brought thousands to a mood of piety, he was still unable to refrain from the kind of conduct that had made him notorious among his undergraduate friends. The authorities in the Church struggled to take a severe view of his misdemeanours, but inevitably at the last moment they could not refrain from smiling. They therefore decided that while some punishment was called for, it should not be too extreme, and the penalty they chose was to make him Bishop of Boria-boola-ga, with the condition that he must never leave his diocese without the express permission of the Archbishops of Canterbury and York. I happened to meet him at this time when an anthropologist was reading a paper on Central African ritual, to which, in the subsequent discussion, the Bishop contributed some trenchant comments. I had always enjoyed his society, and I induced him at the end of the meeting to come with me to my club.

'I believe,' said he, 'that you are a neighbour of a certain Mr. Cartwright, with whom not long ago I had a somewhat curious encounter.'

He then related the circumstances, and wound up with the ominous remark:

'I fear your friend Mr. Cartwright hardly realizes what is in store for him.'

The Bishop had, in fact, been much impressed by Mr. Cartwright's technique, and had wondered whether there was any method by which he could make use of it for the salvation of his black parishioners. At last he hit upon a plan. He took pains to study the Soviet Ambassador, and when he had grasped all his features, gestures, and mannerisms, he hunted among out-of-work actors for one closely resembling that eminent and respected diplomat. Having found one, he induced the man to pose as a fellow-traveller and to get himself invited to a Soviet reception. He then wrote a letter purporting to come from the Ambassador inviting Mr. Cartwright to meet him in a certain hotel. Mr. Cartwright accepted. The apparent Ambassador slipped into his hand a huge envelope, and at the moment at which he received the envelope he heard a sound only too familiar to him—the click of a concealed camera. On looking at the envelope he saw to his horror that it contained in large and clear writing, not only his name, but the superscription 'ten million roubles.' Sure enough, the Bishop came to see him next day, and said:

'Well, my dear friend, you know that imitation is the sincerest flattery, and I have come to flatter you. Here is a photograph quite as good as the one you took of me, and, if I may say so, far more damaging. For I doubt whether the inhabitants of Boria-boola-ga would think much the worse of me for embracing a lovely lady, but the authorities of this great country would certainly think the worse of you if they got a sight of this picture. I do not, however, wish to be too hard upon you, for I have a certain admiration of your ingenuity. I will therefore make easy terms. You must, of course, give me back my I.O.U. and the lien on the revenue of my See, and for so long as you continue the practice of your profession it must be subject to certain conditions. The men whom you blackmail must be only notorious infidels, whose moral downfall, if believed in, will redound to the credit of the true faith. Ninety per cent of any moneys that you receive in this way must be handed over to me.

'You will know that there are still a certain number of heathen in Boria-boola-ga, and that I have a large bet with the neighbouring Bishop of Nyam-Nyam as to who can make the most rapid increase in the number of the faithful in his diocese. I have discovered that all the inhabitants of a village will consent to be baptized if the head man of the village does so. I have discovered also that a head man will consent for the price of three pigs, which is less in Central Africa than it is here. We may perhaps put it at about fifteen pounds. There are still about a thousand head men to be converted. I require, therefore, for the completion of my work the sum of fifteen thousand pounds. When I have acquired this sum through your operations on freethinkers, we shall reconsider our relations. For the present, you shall be free from any unpleasant attentions either on my part or on that of the police.'

Mr. Cartwright, disconcerted, but not yet quite despairing, saw no alternative but to obey the episcopal directions. His first victims were leaders of the Ethical Movement, which exists to maintain that the highest virtue is possible without the help of Christian dogma. His next victims were Communist leaders from the United States, Australia, and other virtuous parts of the world, who had come together to an important conference in London. Before very long, he had succeeded in acquiring the fifteen thousand pounds that the Bishop demanded. The Bishop received the sum in a reverent spirit, and expressed his thankfulness that he would now be able to extirpate paganism in his hitherto benighted diocese.

'And now,' said Mr. Cartwright, 'you will, I am sure, admit that I have earned freedom from your further attentions.'

'Not so fast,' said the Bishop, 'I still possess the original photograph upon which our compact was based. I can, without the slightest difficulty, supply the police with legal evidence of the methods by which you have collected the fifteen thousand pounds that you have handed to me, and you have no evidence whatever that I was in any degree a party to your practices. I cannot see that you have any claim to freedom from my demands.

'I am, however, as I said before, a merciful master, and though you will remain my slave, I will not make your bondage intolerable. There are still two things that are amiss in Boria-boola-ga; one is that the Head Chief still obstinately clings to the faith of his ancestors, and the other is that the population is less than that of Nyam-Nyam. There is a method by which you and your beautiful assistant can remedy both these defects. I have sent her photograph to the Head Chief, and he has fallen madly in love with it. I have given him to understand that if he will become a convert I can secure that she will become his wife. And as for your part, I shall demand that you take up your residence in Boria-boola-ga, and that you shall have a large dusky harem. You shall devote yourself, while your powers last, to begetting souls whom I shall baptize, and if at any time any neglect of your duties becomes apparent through a fall in the birth-rate in your harem, your criminal activities shall be made known.

'I will not say that this is a life sentence. When you reach the age of seventy, you and the exquisite Lalage, perhaps by that time no longer exquisite, shall be allowed to return to England, and to pick up such livelihood as is to be obtained from passport photography. Lest you should think of illegal violence as a way of escape, I must inform you that I have left a sealed envelope at my bank, with orders that it is to be opened if at any time I die in a manner capable of arousing suspicion. This envelope, once opened, will

ensure your ruin. Meanwhile I look forward with much pleasure to the enjoyment of your company in our joint exile. Good morning.'

Mr. Cartwright found no escape from this painful situation. The last time I saw him was at the docks, as he was embarking for Africa. He was bidding a heartbroken farewell to Miss Scraggs, whom the Bishop was compelling to travel by a different ship. I could not but feel some sympathy, but I consoled myself with the thought of the indubitable benefits to the spread of the Gospel.

v

Amid all the troubles of Mr. Abercrombie, Mr. Beauchamp, and Mr. Cartwright, I had not lost sight of Mrs. Ellerker. Indeed events had occurred in connection with her which had caused me much anxiety.

Mr. Ellerker was a designer of aeroplanes, and was considered by the Ministry to be one of the ablest men in this department.

He had only one rival, Mr. Quantox, who, as it happened, also lived in Mortlake. Some authorities considered Mr. Ellerker the abler man, some preferred the work of Mr. Quantox, but no one else in England was considered to reach so high a standard of ability in their field. Except professionally, however, the two men were widely divergent. Mr. Ellerker was a man of narrowly scientific education, unacquainted with literature, indifferent to the arts, pompous in conversation, and addicted to heavy platitudes. Mr. Quantox, on the contrary, was sparkling and witty, a man of wide education and wide culture, a man who could amuse any company by observations which combined wit with penetrating analysis. Mr. Ellerker had never looked at any woman but his wife; Mr. Quantox, on the other hand, had a roving eye, and would have incurred moral reprobation but for the national value of his work, which, like Nelson's, compelled the moralists to pretend ignorance. Mrs. Ellerker, in many of these respects, bore more resemblance to Mr. Quantox than to her husband. Her father was Reader in Anthropology in one of our older universities; she had spent her youth in the most intelligent society to be found in England; she was accustomed to the combination of wit with wisdom, and of both with an absence of the ponderous moralism which Mr. Ellerker retained from the Victorian age. Her neighbours in Mortlake were divided into those who enjoyed her sparkling talk, and those who feared that such lightness in word could not be wedded to perfect correctness in behaviour. The more earnest and elderly among her acquaintance darkly suspected her of moral lapses skilfully concealed, and were inclined to pity Mr. Ellerker for having such a flighty wife. The other faction pitied Mrs. Ellerker, as they imagined his comments on *The Times* leaders at breakfast.

After Mrs. Ellerker's dramatic departure from the house of Dr. Mallako, I made a point of cultivating her acquaintance in the hope that sooner or later I might be of use to her. When I came to know Dr. Mallako's part in the misfortunes of Mr. Abercrombie, I felt it my duty to warn her against him, but this I found unnecessary, since she vehemently repudiated any thought of further acquaintance with him. A new anxiety soon beset me in relation to her. It came to be known that she and Mr. Quantox were meeting more frequently perhaps than was wise in view of the rivalry between him and Mr. Ellerker. Mr. Quantox, in spite of the charm of his conversation, seemed to me a dangerous acquaintance for one in the unstable condition in which Mrs. Ellerker had been left by the impact of Dr. Mallako. I hinted something to this effect in the course of a conversation with her, but her reaction was quite different from what it had been in the case of Dr. Mallako. She flared up, said that gossip was disgusting, and that Mr. Quantox was a man against whom she would not hear a word. So angry did she become that I discontinued my visits to her house, and, in fact, became completely out of touch with her.

So matters remained until one morning, on opening the newspaper, I found terrible news. A plane built to a new model designed by Mr. Ellerker had burst into flames on its trial flight. The pilot had been burnt to death, and an inquiry had been ordered. But worse was to follow. When the police examined Mr. Ellerker's papers they found what appeared to be conclusive evidence that he had been in touch with a foreign Power, and that treachery had led him to deliberate faults in the design of the new plane. When these documents came to light, Mr. Ellerker committed suicide by taking a dose of poison.

Recollections of Dr. Mallako made me doubt whether the truth was quite what it had been made to appear. I visited Mrs. Ellerker, whom I found in a condition not so much of grief as of distraction. I found her afflicted not only with natural sorrow, but with a kind of terror, which at the time I could not understand. In the middle of a sentence she would stop, and seem to be listening, though there was nothing that I could hear. She would then pull herself together with an effort, and say: 'Yes . . . yes . . . what was it we were saying?' and in a half-hearted way take up the conversation where it had been left. I was deeply troubled about her, but she refused at this time to give me her confidence, and I was helpless.

Mr. Quantox, meanwhile, had been marching on to new triumphs. His only rival was gone; the Government depended more and more upon him as their main hope in the armaments race; his name appeared in the Birthday Honours, and his praise was in every newspaper.

For a month or two nothing further happened, until one day I learned from Mr. Gosling that Mrs. Ellerker, in the deepest widow's weeds, had rushed distractedly to the Air Ministry, had insisted wildly that she must see the Minister, and on being shown into his presence had poured forth an incoherent tale, which had appeared to him to be nothing but the product of madness due to grief. He could not quite understand her story, but he gathered that she was bringing incredible accusations against Mr. Quantox, and, incidentally, against herself. An eminent psychiatrist was summoned, and agreed at once that poor Mrs. Ellerker's mind had become unhinged. Mr. Quantox was too valuable a public servant to be at the mercy of a hysterical woman, and Mrs. Ellerker, after being quickly certified, was removed to an asylum.

It so happened that the medical officer in charge of this asylum was an old friend of mine. I went to see him, and asked him, in confidence, to tell me something about the sad case of Mrs. Ellerker. When he had said as much as discretion permitted, I said:

'Dr. Prendergast,' for that was his name, 'I have some knowledge of Mrs. Ellerker's circumstances, and of her social milieu. I think it not impossible that if I am permitted to have an interview with her, without the presence of those attendants who are thought desirable in most mental cases, I may be able to discover the source of her disorder, and perhaps even to point the way towards a cure. I do not say this lightly. There are circumstances known to very few which have a bearing upon the strange occurrences that have brought about Mrs. Ellerker's mental instability. I shall be deeply grateful if you will permit me the opportunity that I seek.'

Dr. Prendergast, after some hesitation, agreed.

I found the poor lady sitting alone and dejected, showing no interest in anything, barely looking up as I entered the room, and giving almost no sign of recognition.

'Mrs. Ellerker,' I said, 'I do not believe that you are suffering from insane delusions. I know Dr. Mallako, and I know Mr. Quantox, and I knew your late husband. I find it quite incredible that Mr. Ellerker should have been guilty of such conduct as has been imputed to him, but I find it wholly credible that Dr. Mallako and Mr. Quantox between them should have brought a good man to destruction. If I am right in my suspicions you can at least rely upon me to give due weight to anything that you may care to tell me, and not to treat it as the delusions of a ruined mind.'

'God bless you for these words,' she replied fervently, 'they are the first that I have heard from which I derive any hope of causing the truth to be believed. Since you are willing to hear my story, I will tell it to you in all its painful details. I must not spare myself, for my part has been one of deep obloquy. But, believe me, I am purged of the evil influence which led me along the downward path, and I wish with all my heart to make such amends as are possible to the besmirched memory of my poor husband.'

With these words she began a long and terrible history.

The whole chain of disaster began, as I had suspected, with the machinations of Dr. Mallako. Mr. Ellerker, having learned that Dr. Mallako was a neighbour of considerable academic distinction, decided that social relations would be in order, and, accompanied by Mrs. Ellerker, paid a call upon that enigmatic personage on the afternoon on which I encountered Mrs. Ellerker fainting at the gate.

After some minutes of desultory conversation, Mr. Ellerker, whose importance was such that the Ministry had always to be informed of his whereabouts, was rung up on the telephone, and told that certain documents in his possession were urgently needed and must be sent immediately by special messenger. He had these documents in his attaché case, and decided that he must go out at once and find a messenger to take them.

'You, my dear,' he said to his wife, 'will perhaps not mind staying with Dr. Mallako during the short time that I shall be absent. When my business is concluded, I will return to fetch you.'

Mrs. Ellerker, who had found Dr. Mallako's conversation more promising than that of most of the inhabitants of Mortlake, was by no means unwilling to have this opportunity of conversation not overshadowed by her husband's pomposities. Dr. Mallako, with a penetration which she vainly endeavoured to resent, had observed the irritation and boredom caused by her husband's lengthy verbosity. What struck her as remarkable, although not at the moment a cause of suspicion, was Dr. Mallako's acquaintance with other people whose circumstances were not unlike her own. He had known, so he said, other designers of aeroplanes, some dull, some interesting. Oddly enough, so he continued, it was the dull ones who had interesting wives.

'You will of course understand, my dear lady,' so he interrupted his story to say, 'that I am merely gossiping about various people that I have happened to meet in the course of my life, and that none of them, so far as I am able to judge, bear any close resemblance to any of the inhabitants of this suburb.

'But in the very brief moments during which I have enjoyed your company, I have already perceived that the human drama is not without interest for you, and I will therefore proceed with my little story.

'I knew at one time two rivals (you will of course understand that this was in another country), one of whom I regret to say was filled with bitter envy of the other's success. The envious one was witty and charming, the other heavy, and without interest in anything outside his work. The envious one (I fear you may find this incredible, but I assure you it is a fact) ingratiated himself with the wife of his less interesting colleague. She fell madly in love with him. She feared that he was less in love with her than she with him. Infatuation drove her on, and at last she told him in a moment of uncontrollable passion that there was no act from which she would shrink if she could thereby win his love. He appeared to hesitate, but after some time he said that there was one quite small thing which she might do for him, a very little thing, so little that she might think it not worth such great preliminaries. Her husband, like other men with similar work, would often bring home with him from the office uncompleted designs to which he wished to put the finishing touches during the small hours. These designs lay on his desk, and while he slept, they were unguarded. Could she, perhaps, without interrupting the worthy man's snores, slip out at break of day, and make such slight changes in the design as her lover would indicate to her from time to time? She could and she would. Her husband, all unconscious of her activities, caused a new plane to be constructed, in accordance with his design as he thought, but in fact with those changes that the wicked lover had indicated. The plane was made; her husband, full of pride in his supposed achievement, took up the plane on its trial flight. It burst into flames and he was killed. The lover, full of gratitude, married her as soon as a decent interval had elapsed. You may have thought, my dear lady,' so Dr. Mallako concluded the tale, 'that some remorse would have dimmed her bliss, but it was not so. So sparkling and delightful was her lover, that never for a single instant did she regret the humdrum husband whom she had sacrificed. Her joy was unclouded, and to this day they are among the happiest couples of my acquaintance.'

At this point Mrs. Ellerker exclaimed in horror: 'There cannot be such wicked women!'

To which Dr. Mallako replied: 'There are some very wicked women in the world—and there are some very boring men.'

Throughout Dr. Mallako's discourse, Mrs. Ellerker, who had hitherto, though with difficulty, lived a virtuous life, found herself obsessed by images which she longed to repress, but could not. She had met Mr. Quantox at various social gatherings. He had shown the most flattering interest in her. He had appeared aware that she had not only charms of person, but a distinguished mind. He had always shown more desire to converse with her than with anyone else in the company. Only now, while Dr. Mallako was talking, she became aware that after such meetings the thought had darted through her mind how different life might be if he were her husband, and not her poor Henry. This thought had been so fleeting and so quickly repressed that until Dr. Mallako's discourse brought it into the open, it had not been sufficiently emphatic to distress her. But now it was out in the open. Now she imagined what she would feel if Mr. Quantox's eyes looked at her with passion, if Mr. Quantox's arms were about her, if Mr. Quantox's lips were in contact with her own. Such thoughts made her tremble, but she could not banish them.

'My mind,' she thought, 'has been decaying in the soporific monotony of Henry's undeviating flatness. His comments on the newspaper at breakfast make me wish to scream. After dinner, when he imagines we have a happy time of leisure, he invariably sleeps, and yet notices at once if I attempt to occupy myself in any way. I do not know how to endure his assumption that I am a sweet and silly little woman, such as he used to read about in adolescence in the bad Victorian novels which he has never outgrown. How different my life would be if it were passed with my dear Eustace, as at least in my dreams I must call Mr. Quantox. How we should stimulate each other, how shine, how make the company marvel at our brilliance! And how he would love, with passion and fire, and yet with a kind of lightness, not with the heaviness of uncooked dough.'

All these thoughts and images rushed through her mind as Dr. Mallako talked. But at the same time another voice, not so loud, not so strident, but nevertheless not without power, reminded her that Mr. Ellerker was a good man, that he did every duty of which he was aware, that his work was distinguished, and his life honourable. Could she, like the wicked woman in Dr. Mallako's story, doom such a man to a painful death?

Torn between duty and desire, she was rocked this way and that by the conflict of passion and compassion. At length, forgetting all about Mr. Ellerker's intended return, she fled wildly from the house, and fainted as she met me at the gate.

Mrs. Ellerker, amid the turmoil of her feelings, would have wished to avoid Mr. Quantox, at any rate until her mind was made up one way or the other. For a few days she took refuge in illness and kept to her bed, but this way out could not last. To her dismay, as soon as she was up and about, Mr. Ellerker said to her:

'Amanda, my dear, now that my little singing bird is restored to health, I wish to ask our neighbour Mr. Quantox to tea. You, of course, do not trouble your pretty head with my professional duties, but Mr. Quantox and I are, in a sense, rivals, and I should wish that there should be between us that civilized behaviour which becomes men of the twentieth century. I think therefore it would be a good plan to ask Mr. Quantox here, and I hope you will do your best to be nice to him—and when you are nice, my dear, few people can be nicer.'

There was no escape. Mr. Quantox came. Mr. Ellerker, as was his wont, retired to his desk and his papers as soon as politeness permitted, saying as he went:

'I am sorry, Mr. Quantox, that public duty prevents me from enjoying any more of your delightful society, but I leave you in good hands. My wife, though not capable of following the intricacies of our somewhat difficult profession, will, I am convinced, be not unable to entertain you for the next half hour or so, if you can tear yourself away for so long a time from those occupations which to us both contain the chief fascination of life.'

When he was gone, Mrs. Ellerker, for a moment, was paralysed by embarrassment, but Mr. Quantox did not allow this mood to continue.

'Amanda,' he said, 'if I may be permitted so to call you, this is the moment for which I have waited since our first meeting at that tedious party, which you alone made tolerable. Who indeed is there in this tiresome suburb with whom either you or I can exchange an intelligent word except each other? I allow myself to hope that you perhaps recognize in me, as I in you, a civilized being, capable of speaking the language that to both of us is natural.'

The rest of his conversation was less personal. He spoke with taste and understanding and knowledge of books and music and pictures, of things which Mr. Ellerker ignored, and Mortlake had never heard of. She forgot her scruples, and as he rose to say goodbye, her eyes were shining.

'Amanda,' he said, 'this has indeed been a delightful half hour. May I hope that some day, some not too distant day, you may be induced to inspect my first editions? I have some which are not unworthy of even your eyes, and it would be a pleasure to show them to one so well able to appreciate them.'

For a moment she hesitated, then, overcome with reckless desire, she agreed, and a date was fixed at a time when Mr. Ellerker was certain to be in his office. Somewhat nervously she rang his bell.

It was he himself who opened the door, and she realized that they were alone in the house. He led the way to his library, and as soon as the door was shut, he took her in his arms. . . .

When at last she tore herself away, in the realization that dear Henry was about to return, and would expect to greet her playfully with the question: 'Well, and what has my little singing bird been doing in the absence of its mate?' she felt desperately that some bond stronger and more stable than mere passion must be forged if she and her beloved Eustace (as she had learned to call Mr. Quantox) were to have more than a passing affair.

'Eustace,' she said, 'I love you, and there is nothing that I would not do, if it might in any way further your happiness.'

'My dear one,' he replied, 'I could not burden you with my problems. You are to me sunshine and light, and I do not wish you associated in my thoughts with the dismal round of daily toil.'

'Oh, Eustace,' she replied, 'do not think of me so. I am not a butterfly. I am not, as Henry supposes, a little singing bird. I am a woman of intelligence and capacity, capable of sharing in the serious life of even such a one as you. I have enough at home of being treated as a plaything. It is not so that I wish you, my beloved, to treat me.'

Mr. Quantox seemed to hesitate, and then, at last, to make up his mind. With a momentary pang of terror she heard him repeat almost literally the words of Dr. Mallako's 'little story.'

'Well,' he said, 'there is one thing that you could do for me, a very little thing, too little, you may think, for such preliminaries.'

'Oh, what is it, Eustace? Tell me!' she cried.

'Well,' he said, 'I imagine that your husband not infrequently brings home with him uncompleted plans for the construction of new planes. If you were to make some very small and unimportant alterations in these plans, such as I shall suggest to you, you would be serving me, and, I dare to hope, yourself.'

'I will do it,' she said, 'you have but to instruct me!' And with that she hurried from the house.

Mr. Quantox's words had been a ghostly echo of the words in Dr. Mallako's little story. The subsequent days continued the echo of this story, until the day came when her husband, full of triumph, informed her that his new plane was now completed, and was to have its trial flight on the morrow. It was after this that reality began to diverge from Dr. Mallako's story. It was not Mr. Ellerker, but a pilot, that took the plane on its trial flight, and was burnt to death when the plane caught fire. Mr. Ellerker came home in the deepest dejection and despair. When a police inquiry found among his papers evidence of treasonable correspondence with a foreign power, Mrs. Ellerker quickly realized that this evidence had been manufactured by her beloved Eustace, but she held her tongue, even after her husband took poison and died.

Mr. Quantox, left without a rival, rose higher and higher in the public esteem, and was rewarded by a grateful sovereign in the next Birthday Honours. But to Mrs. Ellerker his door remained closed, and if they met in the train or the street he gave her only a distant bow. She had served her purpose. Under the lash of this disdain, her passion died, and was succeeded by remorse, bitter, unavailing, and unendurable. At every turn she seemed to hear her dead Henry's voice uttering the familiar platitudes which, while he lived, she had found intolerable. When the newspaper was filled with the trouble in Persia, she seemed to hear her husband's voice saying: 'Why do they not send a few regiments of soldiers to teach these wretched Asiatics a lesson? I warrant you, they would run fast enough when they saw British uniforms!' When she returned in the evening from disconsolate wanderings in search of a moment's respite from torturing thoughts, she would seem to hear her husband saying: 'Do not overdo it, Amanda. These foggy evenings are not good for you. Your cheeks look pale. It is not for delicate women to weary themselves in this manner. The rough and tumble of life is for men, and we must protect our little treasures from all the rubs and troubles with which our lives are beset.' At every odd moment, in the middle of conversations with neighbours, in shopping, in trains, she would hear his rotund but kindly platitudes whispered into her ear, until she could not believe that he was really absent. She would look round quickly, and people would say: 'What is it, Mrs. Ellerker? You look startled.' And then fear, stark, terrible fear, would take possession of her soul. Every day more insistently the voice whispered; every day the rolling platitudes grew longer; every day the kindly solicitude grew more intolerable.

At last she could bear it no longer. The sight of Mr. Quantox's name in the Birthday Honours was the last straw. She rushed wildly from the house, and tried to tell her tale, but only the silence of the asylum walls was allowed to hear it.

After listening to this dreadful story, I spoke to Dr. Prendergast. I spoke to Mr. Ellerker's chiefs in the Air Ministry. I spoke to all that I thought could be of some use to poor Mrs. Ellerker, but not one auditor did I find who would listen to my story.

'No,' they all replied, 'Sir Eustace is too valuable a public servant. We cannot have his name tarnished. But for him we could not compete with American designers. But for him the Russian planes would out-class us. It may be that the story you have told is true, but whether true or false, it is not in the public interest that it should be known, and we must request you, indeed we must command you, to hold your tongue about it.'

And so Mrs. Ellerker continues to languish, and Mr. Quantox to prosper.

VI

My failure to help Mrs. Ellerker, not only in itself, but in its political implications, was a cause of profound mental disturbance to me. 'Can it indeed be the case,' I thought, 'that these men to whom I have appealed, medical men and statesmen, among the most highly respected individuals in our supposedly decent community, can it be that these men, one and all, are prepared that this poor woman should suffer under an undeserved stigma, while the culprit to whom her misfortunes are due marches on from one honour to another? And for what end are they willing to perpetrate this infamy?' At this point my thoughts became perhaps somewhat unbalanced. Their acts, it seemed to me, had only one end in view, that through the ingenuity of Mr. Quantox many Russians should perish who, but for his ingenuity, might remain alive. In my unwholesome state of mind I did not consider this a sufficient compensation for the unjust treatment of Mrs. Ellerker.

I became increasingly filled with a general detestation of mankind. I surveyed those whom I had known, and they seemed a sorry crew. Mr. Abercrombie was willing to let an innocent man suffer obloquy and prison in order that he and his wife might have the empty pleasure of a trivial title. Mr. Beauchamp was willing to debauch the minds of schoolboys in the hope of pleasing a heartless lady of easy virtue. Mr. Cartwright, although he firmly believed in the pre-eminent merit of those whom the world delights to honour, was nevertheless prepared to cause them shame and misery and financial loss to provide himself with gross luxuries. Mrs. Ellerker, I had to admit, had been guilty, so far as mere acts are concerned, of conduct quite as dreadful as that of Mr. Abercrombie, Mr. Beauchamp, and Mr. Cartwright. But, perhaps inconsistently, I refused to regard her as morally responsible during the period of her crime. I thought of her as the hapless victim of Dr. Mallako and Mr. Quantox, acting in a sinister harmony. But, like the Lord when he plotted the destruction of Sodom, I did not consider that one exception was enough to earn a respite for the human race.

'Dr. Mallako,' so my thoughts went in this gloomy and dreadful time, 'Dr. Mallako is the prince of the world because in him, in his malignant mind, in his cold destructive intellect, are concentrated in quintessential form all the baseness, all the cruelty, all the helpless rage of feeble men aspiring to be Titans. Dr. Mallako is wicked, granted, but why is his wickedness successful? Because in many who are timidly respectable there lurks the hope of splendid sin, the wish to dominate and the urge to destroy. It is to these secret passions that he makes his appeal, and it is to them that he owes his dreadful power.

'Mankind,' I thought, 'are a mistake. The universe would be sweeter and fresher without them. When the morning dew sparkles like diamonds in the rising sun of a September morning, there is beauty and exquisite purity in each blade of grass, and it is dreadful to think of this beauty being beheld by sinful eyes, which smirch its loveliness with their sordid and cruel ambitions. I cannot understand how God, who sees this loveliness, can have tolerated so long the baseness of those who boast blasphemously that they have been made in His image. Perhaps,' I thought, 'it may yet fall to my lot to be the more thoroughgoing instrument of the Divine Purpose which was carried out half-heartedly in the days of Noah.'

My physical researches had shown me various ways in which human life might be brought to an end. I could not but think it my duty to carry one of these means to its completion. Of all those that I had discovered, the easiest appeared to be a new chain reaction by which the sea could be made to boil. I concocted an apparatus which, so far as I could see, would achieve this purpose whenever I chose. Only one thing held me back, and that was that, while men would die of thirst, fishes would die of being boiled. I had nothing against fishes, which, so far as I then knew, and so far as I had observed in aquariums, were harmless and pleasant creatures, not infrequently beautiful, and possessed of a far from human dexterity in the avoidance of impacts with each other.

In a nominally jocular spirit I spoke to a zoological colleague about the possibility of making the sea boil. And I said, laughing, that perhaps it would be rather hard upon the fishes. My friend entered into the spirit of the supposed joke.

'I shouldn't worry about the fishes, if I were you,' he said. 'I can assure you that the wickedness of fishes is appalling. They eat each other; they neglect their young; and their sexual habits are such as bishops pronounce gravely sinful when practised by human beings. I do not see that you need have any remorse in causing the death of sharks.'

Little as he knew it, this man's jesting words determined me. 'It is not only man,' so my thoughts ran, 'that is rapacious and cruel. It is part of the very nature of life, or at least of animal life, since it can only live by preying upon other life. Life itself is evil. Let the planet become dead like the moon, and it will then be as beautiful and as innocent.'

With great secrecy I set to work. After some failures I made an apparatus which, I was persuaded, would cause first the Thames, then the North Sea, then the Atlantic and the Pacific, and, last of all, even the frozen Polar Oceans, to boil away into futile steam. 'As this happens,' so ran my somewhat disordered thoughts, 'as this happens, the earth will grow hotter and hotter, men's thirst will increase, and, in a universal shriek of madness, they will perish. Then,' I thought, 'there will be no more Sin.' I will not deny that in this vast vision my thoughts reserved a quite special place for the downfall of Dr. Mallako. I imagined his mind to be full of ingenious schemes for becoming the Emperor of the world, and imposing his will upon reluctant victims, whose torments should increase for him the sweet savour of their submission. In imagination I enjoyed triumph over that wicked man, a triumph achieved perhaps by what some might think a wickedness even greater than his own, but redeemed by the clean purity of a noble passion. While these thoughts boiled within me, as terribly as in my hopes the sea was about to boil, I completed my apparatus and attached it to a clockwork mechanism. One morning at ten o'clock I set the mechanism. The sea was to boil at noon. And having set the mechanism, I paid a last and final visit to Dr. Mallako.

Dr. Mallako, who was well aware that my feelings towards him were not wholly friendly, was somewhat surprised by my call.

'To what,' he said, 'do I owe the honour of this visit?'

'Doctor,' I replied, 'this, as you surmise, is no mere social call. It is useless for you to offer me your whisky, or your comfortable chair. It is not for a pleasant chat that I have come. I have come to tell you that your reign is at an end, that the evil sway which you have exercised over the minds and hearts of those who have had the misfortune of your acquaintance is to cease from this time forth, and is to cease through a combination of intelligence and courage as great as your own, but devoted to a nobler end. I, the poor despised scientist, whom you considered of no account, whose efforts to thwart the tragedies that you have brought about have hitherto been as unavailing as you could wish, I have at last discovered how to thwart your ambitions. A clock is at this moment ticking in my laboratory, and when the hands of this clock point to midday, a process will be set in motion which, within a few days, will put an end to all life on this planet—and, incidentally, to your life, Dr. Mallako.'

'Dear me,' said Dr. Mallako, 'how very melodramatic! It is too early in the morning for me to suppose that you have been drinking, and I am therefore compelled to suppose some graver derangement of your mental faculties. But if you find the matter of sufficient interest, I shall be delighted to listen while you expound your scheme for producing this slightly catastrophic result.'

'It is all very well,' I replied, 'for you to sneer. It is perhaps all that is left for you to do. But soon your sneers will be stilled, and as you perish, you will be forced to admit, with whatever bitterness of defeat, that the ultimate triumph is mine.'

'Come, come,' said Dr. Mallako, with some impatience, 'enough of this rodomontade. If indeed only a few hours remain to us, how can we spend them better than in intelligent converse? Tell me your scheme, and I will see what I think of it. I will confess that as yet I am not much alarmed. You were always a bungler. What did you achieve for Mr. Abercrombie, or Mr. Beauchamp, or Mr. Cartwright, or Mrs. Ellerker? Are any of them the better for your protection, and will the human race be any the worse for your enmity? But, come, tell me your plan. It may be that failure has sharpened your wits, though I doubt it.'

I could not resist this invitation. I was confident in my invention, and determined to have the laugh on the contemptuous Doctor. The principle upon which I had operated was simple, and the Doctor's wits were nimble. Within a few minutes he had grasped both my theory and my practice. But, alas, the result was not what I had hoped.

'My poor fellow,' he said, 'it is just as I had supposed. You have overlooked one small point, which makes it certain that your apparatus will not work. When twelve o'clock strikes your clock will blow up, and the sea will remain as cold as before.'

In a few simple words he demonstrated the truth of what he had said. Deflated and miserable, I prepared to take my departure.

'Wait a minute,' he said, 'do not imagine that all is lost. Hitherto we have worked against each other, but perhaps if you will deign to accept my help something of your curious hopes may yet be salvaged. While you were talking I not only perceived the flaw in your apparatus, but also a method of remedying it. I shall now have no difficulty in constructing a machine which will do what you thought yours would do. You fondly imagined that the destruction of the world would be a grief to me. You little know. You have seen so far only the outer fringes of my mind. But in view of our peculiar relations, I will pay you the compliment of taking you somewhat further into my confidence.

'You have imagined that I wanted riches and power and glory for myself. It is not so. I have been always disinterested, never out for myself, but always pursuing aims that were impersonal and abstract. You imagine in your miserable way that you hate mankind. But there is a thousand times more hate in my little finger than in your whole body. The flame of hate that burns within me would shrivel you to ashes in a moment. You have not the strength, the endurance, the will, to live with such hate as mine. If I had known sooner what, thanks to you, I now know, the means to bring about universal death, do you suppose I should have hesitated? Death has been my aim throughout. I have been merely practising on the wretched individuals who roused your silly compassion. Always greater things have lain before me. Have you ever asked yourself why I helped Mr. Quantox towards his triumphs? Have you known (I am sure you have not) that I am giving equal help to his adversaries, who are designing engines of destruction to be used against him and his friends? You have not realized (how indeed should you, having an imagination of so paltry a scope?), you have not realized that revenge is the guiding motive of my life—revenge not against this man or that, but against the whole vile race to which I have the misfortune to belong.

'Very early in my life I conceived this purpose. My father was a Russian prince, my mother a slavey in a London lodging house. My father deserted her before I was born and became a waiter in a New York restaurant. He is now, I believe, enjoying the hospitality of Sing Sing. But he is of little interest to me, and I have not troubled to verify the sources of my information. My mother, after he had deserted her, sought alcoholic consolation. Throughout my early childhood I was always hungry. As soon as I could toddle, I learned to rummage in dust heaps for crusts of bread or potato peelings or anything else from which some scrap of nourishment was to be derived. But my mother objected to these wanderings, and when she remembered, she would lock me up while she visited the public house. When she returned, completely intoxicated, she would knock me about till I bled, and at last stunned me into insensibility to stop my cries. One day, when I was about six years old, as she was drunkenly dragging me along the street, she set to work to give me wanton blows. I dodged. She overbalanced, and a passing lorry put an end to her life.

'A philanthropic lady, who happened to be passing, seeing me left alone and helpless, took pity on me. She brought me to her home, washed me and fed me. My intelligence had been sharpened by misfortunes, and I exerted myself to augment her benevolent pity to the utmost. In this I was wholly successful. She was persuaded that I was a good little boy. She adopted me, and educated me. For the sake of these benefits, I put up with the almost intolerable boredom that she inflicted upon me in the shape of prayers and church-goings and moral sentiments, and a twittering sentimental softness to which I longed to retort with something biting and bitter, with which to wither her foolish optimism. All these impulses I restrained. To please her I would go on my knees and flatter my Maker, though I was at a loss to see what He had to be proud of in making me. To please her I would express a gratitude which I did not feel. To please her I would seem always what she considered "good." At last when I reached the age of twenty-one she made a will leaving me all her property. After this, as you may imagine, she did not live long.

'Since her death my material circumstances have been easy, but never for one moment have I been able to forget those early years —the cruelty of my mother, the heartlessness of neighbours, the hunger, the friendlessness, the dark despair, the complete absence of hope—all these things, in spite of subsequent good fortune, have remained the very texture of my life. There is no human being, no, not one, whom I do not hate. There is no being, no, not one, whom I do not wish to see suffering the absolute extremity of torment. You have offered me the spectacle of the whole population of the globe maddened with thirst, and dying in agonies of futile frenzy. What a delicious spectacle! Were I capable of gratitude I should feel some to you now, and should be tempted to think of you as almost a friend. But the capacity for such feelings died in me before I reached the age of six. You are, I will admit, a convenience to me, but more than that I will not admit.

'You will go home and see your silly machine explode harmlessly. You will know that I, I over whom you thought to triumph, I whom frivolously and absurdly you chose to think worse than yourself, that I am going to achieve the ultimate triumph which you had reserved for yourself, and, so far from hindering my plans, you have supplied the one thing lacking to my perfect triumph. And as you die of thirst, you need not think that I shall be suffering equal torments. When I have set the inexorable machinery in motion I shall die painlessly. But you will be left for a few hours, perhaps for a few days, to writhe in ignoble agony, knowing that in my last moments I shall have rejoiced in the prospect.'

But as he talked, my thoughts went through a sudden revulsion. That he was wicked was my most profound belief. If he wished to destroy the world, then it must be wicked to destroy the world. When I had thought that I would destroy it, I had enjoyed the vision of cleansing power. When I thought that he would destroy it, I had only a vision of diabolic hate. I could not permit his triumph. The world which I had been hating began, as he talked, to seem beautiful. The hatred of human beings, which was the very breath of his being, was in me, as I now saw, only a passing madness. I determined that for all his proud words he should be defeated. For a moment he looked out of the window, and exclaimed:

'How many houses can be seen from here! Out of each of these houses, not many days from now, shrieking maniacs will rush. I shall not see it, but in my mind's eye, as I die, the delicious panorama will be unfolded.'

While he said this, his back was to me. I whipped out the revolver which I had brought in case of violence.

'No!' I said, 'this will not happen.'

He turned round, with an angry sneer, and as he turned I shot him dead. I first wiped the revolver, then, putting on gloves, I pressed his fingers round it, and left it lying near him. I quickly typed a suicide note on his typewriter. In this note I made him say: 'I find that I am not the man of iron will that I had hoped I was. I have sinned, and remorse is devouring me. My latest schemes were on the point of failure, and I should have been disgraced and ruined. I cannot face this, and I die by my own hand.'

I then went home and disconnected my useless machine, just in time to prevent a paltry explosion.

### VII

For some time after putting an end to Dr. Mallako, I felt happy and carefree. From him, I thought, had emanated a kind of poisonous miasma, infecting with crime or madness or disaster all in his neighbourhood. And now that he was gone, it should be possible to live freely and joyously, to prosper in my work, and be peaceful in my personal relations. For some months I slept as I had not slept since the day when Dr. Mallako's brass plate first met my eyes, dreamlessly, refreshingly, and sufficiently. From time to time, it is true, I was visited by recollections of poor Mrs. Ellerker, living among lunatics, desolate and alone. But I had done all that I could for her, and nothing was to be gained by further brooding. I determined that I would resolutely banish all thought of her from my life.

I met a charming and intelligent lady, who at first captured my attention by her knowledge of the more devious paths of psychiatry. Here, I thought, is someone who, should the need ever arise, as, please God, it will not, will be able to follow the strange convolutions of evil through which it has been my misfortune to thread my way. After a not unduly protracted courtship, I married this lady and believed myself happy. But still at times strange disquieting thoughts would come into my mind, some expression of horrified perplexity would pass over my face in the middle of a conversation about everyday matters.

'What is it?' my wife would say, 'some troubling vision seems to have occurred to you. Perhaps you would be the better for telling it.'

'No,' I would reply, 'it is nothing, only some rather tiresome memory which inadvertently interrupted my planning.'

But I observed with alarm that these thoughts came with increasing frequency and continually increasing vividness. I found myself in imagination holding colloquy with Dr. Mallako, continuing the argument of the last hour of his life. For a moment his quietly contemptuous face would appear before me in vivid, visualized detail, and I would seem to hear his sneering voice saying: 'You think I'm defeated, do you?' If this occurred when I was alone in my study, I would shout: 'Yes, I do, damn you!' and once, when I was shouting this, my wife came in at the door and looked strangely at me.

Oftener and oftener I felt his imagined presence. 'You have not been much good to Mrs. Ellerker, have you?' I would hear him saying. 'You think you have recovered your sanity, do you?' I should seem to hear him whisper. My work suffered because, whenever I was alone, I could not banish from my mind the phrases that I fancied he would use: 'Fine ideas you used to have about destroying the world and all that, and now look at you! As humdrum and respectable a man as is to be found in Mortlake. Do you really imagine that you can escape my power by the help of a mere revolver? Do you not know that my power is spiritual and rests unshakably upon the weakness in yourself? If you were half the man that you pretended to be in our last little talk you would confess what you have done. Confess? Nay, boast. You would explain to the world of what a monster you had rid it. You would boast yourself a hero, one who in single combat had worsted the forces of evil concentrated in my wicked person. Did you do any of this? You did not. You left an unavailing and lying pretended confession, attributing contemptible weakness to me—ME—whom alone of mankind weakness has never approached! Do you think that this can be forgiven you? Had you boasted of your deeds I might perhaps have thought you no unworthy adversary. But in this snivelling garb of matrimonial insignificance you have become to me an object of such contempt that, though I be dead, yet I must still show that I can destroy you.'

All this I fancied him saying. At first I knew it was fancy, but as time went on I came more and more to feel that his terrible ghost was real. I would even seem to see him standing before me with his correct black clothes and his smooth, oily hair. Once in a frenzy I walked straight through the apparition in order to persuade myself that it was an apparition, but in the dreadful moment in which it enveloped me completely I felt such a chill breath upon me that I all but shrieked and fainted. My wife, finding me pale and trembling, inquired after me with anxiety. I assured her that river mists had given me an ague, but I could see that she doubted whether this were all. When the ghost taunted me with having concealed my part in his death I began to think that perhaps, if I confessed all, he would let me be.

In dreams I re-enacted the scene in which I had shot him, but with a different ending. In my dreams, when his corpse lay at my feet, I threw open his window, and called out into the street: 'Come up, come up, all you who live in Mortlake! Come up and behold a dead fiend, dead by my heroic act!' So the scene ended in my dream. But when I awoke, there was the sneering ghost saying: 'Ha ha!—that was not quite what you did, was it?'

The torment grew gradually worse, the haunting more continual. Last night the climax came. After a dream even more vivid than usual I awoke shouting: 'I did it. It was I.'

'What did you do?' asked my wife, awakened from sleep by my shout.

'I killed Dr. Mallako,' I told her. 'You may have thought that you had married a humdrum scientific worker, but it is not so. You married a man who, with a rare courage, with determination and with an insight possessed by none among the other inhabitants of this suburb, pursued a cruel fiend to his last end. I killed Dr. Mallako, and I am proud of it!'

'There, there,' said my wife, 'hadn't you better go to sleep again?'

I raged and stormed, but my raging and storming were of no avail. I saw fear overcoming all other feelings in her. As morning came I heard her go to the telephone.

Now, looking out of my window, I see on the door-step two policemen, and an eminent psychiatrist whom I have long known. I see that the same fate awaits me as that from which I failed to save Mrs. Ellerker. Nothing stretches before me but long dreary years of solitude and misunderstanding. Only one feeble ray of light pierces the gloom of my future. Once a year, the better behaved among male and female lunatics are allowed to meet at a well-patrolled dance. Once a year I shall meet my dear Mrs. Ellerker, whom I ought never to have tried to forget, and when we meet, we will wonder whether there will ever be in the world more than two sane people.

# THE CORSICAN ORDEAL OF MISS X

I

I had occasion recently to visit my good friend, Professor N, whose paper on pre-Celtic Decorative Art in Denmark raised some points that I felt needed discussing. I found him in his study, but his usually benign and yet slightly intelligent expression was marred by some strange bewilderment. The books which should have been on the arm of the chair, and which he supposed himself to be reading, were scattered in confusion on the floor. The spectacles which he imagined to be on his nose lay idle on his desk. The pipe which was usually in his mouth lay smoking in his tobacco bowl, though he seemed completely unaware of its not occupying its usual place. His mild and somewhat silly philanthropy and his usually placid gaze had somehow dropped off him. A harassed, distracted, bewildered, and horrified expression was stamped upon his features.

'Good God!' I said, 'what has happened?'

'Ah,' said he, 'it is my secretary, Miss X. Hitherto, I have found her level-headed, efficient, cool, and destitute of those emotions which are only too apt to distract youth. But in an ill-advised moment I allowed her to take a fortnight's holiday from her labours on decorative art, and she, in a still more ill-advised moment, chose to spend the fortnight in Corsica. When she returned I saw at once that something had happened. "What *did* you do in Corsica?" I asked. "Ah! What indeed!" she replied.'

II

The secretary was not in the room at the moment, and I hoped that Professor N might enlarge a little upon the misfortune that had befallen him. But in this I was disappointed. Not another word, so at least he assured me, had he been able to extract from Miss X. Horror piled upon horror glared from her eyes at the mere recollection, but nothing more specific could he discover.

I felt it my duty to the poor girl, who, so I had been given to understand, had hitherto been hard-working and conscientious, to see whether anything could be done to relieve her of the dreadful weight which depressed her spirits. I bethought me of Mrs. Menhennet, a middle-aged lady of considerable bulk, who, so I was informed by her grandchildren, had once had some pretences to beauty. Mrs. Menhennet, I knew, was the granddaughter of a Corsican bandit; in one of those unguarded moments, too frequent, alas, in that rough island, the bandit had assaulted a thoroughly respectable young lady, with the result that she had given birth, after a due interval, to the redoubtable Mr. Gorman.

Mr. Gorman, though his work took him into the City, pursued there the same kind of activities as had led to his existence. Eminent financiers trembled at his approach. Well-established bankers of unblemished reputation had ghastly visions of prison. Merchants who imported the wealth of the gorgeous East turned pale at the thought of Customs House officers at the dead of night. All of which misfortunes, it was well understood, were set in motion by the machinations of the predacious Mr. Gorman.

His daughter, Mrs. Menhennet, would have heard of any strange and unwonted disturbance in the home of her paternal grandfather. I therefore asked for an interview, which was graciously accorded. At four o'clock on a dark afternoon in November I presented myself at her tea-table.

'And what,' she said, 'brings you here? Do not pretend that it is my charms. The day for such pretence is past. For ten years it would have been true; for another ten I should have believed it. Now it is neither true nor do I believe it. Some other motive brings you here, and I palpitate to know what it may be.'

This approach was somewhat too direct for my taste. I find a pleasure in a helicoidal approach to my subject. I like to begin at a point remote from that at which I am aiming, or on occasion, if I begin at a point near my ultimate destination, I like to approach the actual point by a boomerang course, taking me at first away from the final mark and thereby, I hope, deceiving my auditor. But Mrs. Menhennet would permit no such finesse. Honest, downright, and straightforward, she believed in the direct approach, a characteristic which she seemed to have inherited from her Corsican grandfather. I therefore abandoned all attempt at circumlocution and came straight to the core of my curiosity.

'Mrs. Menhennet,' I said, 'it has come to my knowledge that there have been in recent weeks strange doings in Corsica, doings which, as I can testify from ocular demonstration, have turned brown hairs grey and young springy steps leaden with the weariness of age. These doings, I am convinced, owing to certain rumours which have reached me, are of transcendent international importance. Whether some new Napoleon is marching to the conquest of Moscow, or some younger Columbus to the discovery of a still unknown Continent, I cannot guess. But something of this sort, I am convinced, is taking place in those wild mountains, something of the sort is being plotted secretly, darkly, dangerously, something of the sort is being concealed tortuously, ferociously and criminally from those who rashly seek to pierce the veil. You, dear lady, I am convinced, in spite of the correctness of your tea-table and the elegance of your china and the fragrance of your Lapsang Souchong, have not lost touch with the activities of your revered father. At his death, I know, you made yourself the guardian of those interests for which he stood. His father, who had ever been to him a shining light on the road towards swift success, inspired every moment of his life. Since his death, although perhaps some of your less perspicacious friends may not have pierced your very efficient disguise, you, I know, have worn his mantle. You, if anyone in this cold and dismal city, can tell me what is happening in that land of sunshine, and what plots, so dark as to cause eclipse even in the blaze of noon, are being hatched in the minds of those noble descendants of ancient greatness. Tell me, I pray you, what you know. The life of Professor N, or if not his life at least his reason, is trembling in the balance. He is, as you are well aware, a benevolent man, not fierce like you and me, but full of gentle loving-kindness. Owing to this trait in his character he cannot divest himself of responsibility for the welfare of his worthy secretary, Miss X, who returned yesterday from Corsica transformed completely from the sunny carefree girl that once she was to a lined, harassed and weary woman weighed down by all the burdens of the world. What it was that happened to her she refuses to reveal, but if it cannot be discovered it is much to be feared that that great genius, which has already all but solved the many and intricate problems besetting the interpretation of pre-Celtic decorative art, will totter and disintegrate and fall a heap of rubble, like the old Campanile in Venice. You cannot, I am sure, be otherwise than horrified at such a prospect, and I therefore beseech you to unfold, so far as lies in your power, the dreadful secrets of your ancestral home.'

Mrs. Menhennet listened to my words in silence, and when I ceased to speak she still for a while abstained from all reply. At a certain point in my discourse the colour faded from her cheeks and she gave a great gasp. With an effort she composed herself, folded her hands, and compelled her breathing to become quiet.

'You put before me,' she said, 'a dreadful dilemma. If I remain silent, Professor N, not to mention Miss X, must be deprived of reason. But if I speak. . . .' Here she shuddered, and no further word emerged.

At this point, when I had been at a loss to imagine what the next development would be, the parlour-maid appeared and mentioned that the chimney-sweep, in full professional attire, was waiting at the door, as he had been engaged to sweep the chimney of the drawing-room that very afternoon.

'Good heavens!' she exclaimed. 'While you and I have been engaged in small talk and trivial badinage this proud man with his great duties to perform has been kept waiting at my doorstep. This will never do. For now this interview must be at an end. One last word, however. I advise you, if you are in earnest, but only if you are, to pay a visit to General Prz.'[1]

III

General Prz, as everybody remembers, greatly distinguished himself in the First World War by his exploits in defence of his native Poland. Poland, however, in recent years had shown herself ungrateful, and he had been compelled to take refuge in some less unsettled country. A long life of adventure had made the old man, in spite of his grey hairs, unwilling to sink into a quiet life. Although admirers offered him a villa at Worthing, a bijou residence at Cheltenham, or a bungalow in the mountains of Ceylon, none of these took his fancy. Mrs. Menhennet gave him an introduction to some of the more unruly of her relatives in Corsica, and among them he found once more something of the *élan*, the fire and the wild energy which had inspired the exploits of his earlier years.

But although Corsica remained his spiritual home, and his physical home during the greater part of the year, he would allow himself on rare occasions to visit such of the capitals of Europe as were still west of the Iron Curtain. In these capitals he would

[1] Pronounced 'Pish'

converse with the elder statesmen, who would anxiously ask his opinion on all the major trends of recent policy. Whatever he deigned to say in reply they listened to with the respect justly owing to his years and valour. And he would carry back to his mountain fastness the knowledge of the part that Corsica—yes, even Corsica—could play in the great events to come.

As the friend of Mrs. Menhennet, he was at once admitted to the innermost circle of those who, within or without the law, kept alive the traditions of ancient liberty which their Ghibelline ancestors had brought from the still vigorous republics of Northern Italy. In the deep recesses of the hills, hidden from the view of the casual tourist, who saw nothing but rocks and shepherds' huts and a few stunted trees, he was allowed to visit old palaces full of medieval splendour, the armour of ancient Gonfalonieri, and the jewelled swords of world-famous Condottieri. In their magnificent halls these proud descendants of ancient chieftains assembled and feasted, not perhaps always wisely but always too well. Even in converse with the General their lips were sealed as to some of the great secrets of their order, except indeed, in those moments of exuberant conviviality, when the long story of traditional hospitality overcame the scruples which at other times led to a prudent silence.

It was in these convivial moments that the General learned of the world-shaking design that these men cherished, a design that inspired all their waking actions and dominated the dreams in which their feasts too often terminated. Nothing loath, he threw himself into their schemes with all the ardour and all the traditional recklessness of the ancient Polish nobility. He thanked God that at a period of life when to most men nothing remains but reminiscence he had been granted the opportunity to share in great deeds of high adventure. On moonlight nights he would gallop over the mountains on his great charger, whose sire and dam alike had helped him to shed immortal glory upon the stricken fields of his native land. Inspired by the rapid motion of the night wind, his thoughts flowed through a mingled dream of ancient valour and future triumph, in which past and future blended in the alembic of his passion.

At the time when Mrs. Menhennet uttered her mysterious suggestion it happened that the General was engaged in one of his periodic rounds of visits to the elder statesmen of the Western world. He had in the past entertained a somewhat anachronistic prejudice against the Western hemisphere, but since he had learned from his island friends that Columbus was a Corsican he had endeavoured to think better than before of the consequences of that adventurer's somewhat rash activities. He could not quite bring himself actually to imitate Columbus, since he felt that there would be a slight taint of trade about any such journey, but he would call after due notice on the American Ambassador to the Court of St. James's, who always took pains to have a personal message from the President in readiness for his distinguished guest. He would, of course, visit Mr. Winston Churchill, but he never demeaned himself so far as to recognize the existence of Socialist ministers.

It was after he had been dining with Mr. Churchill that I had the good fortune to find him at leisure in the ancient club of which he was an honorary member. He honoured me with a glass of his pre-1914 Tokay, which was part of the *spolia opima* of his encounter with the eminent Hungarian general whom he left dead upon the field of honour with a suitable eulogy for his bravery. After due acknowledgment of the great mark of favour which he was bestowing upon me—a notable mark, for after all not even Hungarian generals go into battle with more than a few bottles of Tokay bound to their saddles—I led the conversation gradually towards Corsica.

'I have heard,' I said, 'that that island is not what it was. Education, they tell me, has turned brigands into bank clerks, and stilettos into stylographic pens. No longer, so they tell me, do ancient vendettas keep alive through the generations. I have even heard dreadful tales of intermarriage between families which had had a feud lasting eight hundred years, and yet the marriage was not accompanied by bloodshed. If all this is indeed true, I am forced to weep. I had always hoped, if fortune should favour my industry, to exchange the sanitary villa which I inhabit in Balham for some stormy peak in the home of ancient romance. But if romance even there is dead, what remains to me as a hope for old age? Perhaps you can reassure me; perhaps something yet lingers there. Perhaps amid thunder and lightning the ghost of Farinata degli Uberti is still to be seen looking around with great disdain. I have come to you tonight in the hope that you can give me such reassurance, since without it I shall not know how to support the burden of the humdrum years.'

As I was speaking his eyes gleamed. I saw him clench his fists and close his jaws fiercely. Scarcely could he wait for the end of my periods. And as soon as I was silent he burst forth.

'Young man,' he said, 'were you not a friend of Mrs. Menhennet I should grudge you that noble nectar which I have allowed your unworthy lips to consume. I am compelled to think that you have been associating with the ignoble. Some few there may be among the riff-raff of the ports, and the ignoble gentry who concern themselves with the base business of bureaucracy—some few there may be, I repeat, of whom the dreadful things at which you have been hinting may be true. But they are no true Corsicans. They are but bastard Frenchmen, or gesticulating Italians, or toadeating Catalans. The true Corsican breed is what it always was. It lives the free life, and emissaries of governments who seek to interfere die the death. No, my friend, all is yet well in that happy home of heroism.'

I leapt to my feet and took his right hand in both of mine.

'O happy day,' said I, 'when my faith is restored, and my doubts are quenched! Would that I might see with my own eyes the noble breed of men whom you have brought so forcibly before my imagination. Could you permit me to know even one of them I should live a happier life, and the banalities of Balham would become more bearable.'

'My young friend,' said he, 'your generous enthusiasm does you credit. Great though the favour may be, I am willing, in view of your enthusiasm, to grant the boon you ask. You shall know one of these splendid survivors of the golden age of man. I know that one of them, indeed one of my closest friends among them—I speak of the Count of Aspramonte—will be compelled to descend from the hills to pick up in Ajaccio a consignment of new saddles for his stallions. These saddles, you will of course understand, are made specially for him by the man who has charge of the racing stables of the Duke of Ashby-de-la-Zouche. The Duke is an old friend of mine, and as a great favour allows me occasionally to purchase from him a few saddles for the use of such of my friends as I deem worthy of so priceless a gift. If you care to be in Ajaccio next week, I can give you a letter to the Count of Aspramonte, who would be more accessible there than in his mountain fastness.'

With tears in my eyes I thanked him for his great kindness. I bowed low and kissed his hand. As I left his presence, my heart was filled with sorrow at the thought of the nobility that is perishing from our ignoble earth.

IV

Following the advice of General Prz, I flew the following week to Ajaccio, and inquired at the principal hotels for the Count of Aspramonte. At the third place of inquiry I was informed that he was at the moment occupying the imperial suite, but that he was a busy man with little time for unauthorized visitors. From the demeanour of the hotel servants I inferred that he had earned their most profound respect. In an interview with the proprietor I handed over the letter of introduction from General Prz with the request that it should be put as soon as possible into the hands of the Count of Aspramonte, who, I learned, was at the moment engaged in business in the town.

The hotel was filled with a chattering throng of tourists of the usual description, all of them, so far as I could observe, trivial and transitory. Coming fresh from the dreams of General Prz I felt the atmosphere a strange one, by no means such as I could have wished. It was not in this setting that I could imagine the realization of the Polish nobleman's dreams. I had, however, no other clue, and was compelled to make the best of it.

After an ample dinner, totally indistinguishable from those provided in the best hotels of London, New York, Calcutta and Johannesburg, I was sitting somewhat disconsolate in the lounge, when I saw approaching me a brisk gentleman of young middle age whom I took at first to be a successful American executive. He had the square jaw, the firm step and the measured speech which I have learned to associate with that powerful section of society. But to my surprise, when he addressed me it was in English English with a continental accent. To my still greater surprise he mentioned that he was the Count of Aspramonte.

'Come,' he said, 'to the sitting-room of my suite, where we can talk more undisturbed than in this mêlée.'

His suite, when we reached it, turned out to be ornate and palatial in a somewhat garish style. He gave me a stiff whisky and soda and a large cigar.

'You are, I see,' so he began the conversation, 'a friend of that dear old gentleman, General Prz. I hope you have never been tempted to laugh at him. For us who live in the modern world the temptation undoubtedly exists, but out of respect for his grey hairs I resist it.

'You and I, my dear Sir,' he continued, 'live in the modern world and have no use for memories and hopes that are out of place in an age dominated by dollars. I for my part, although I live in a somewhat out of the way part of the world, and although I might, if I let myself be dominated by tradition, be as lost in misty dreams as the worthy General, have decided to adapt myself to our time. The main purpose of my life is the acquisition of dollars, not only for myself but for my island. "How," you may ask, "does your manner of life conduce to this end?" In view of your friendship with the General I feel that I owe you an answer to this not unnatural query.

'The mountains in which I have my home afford an ideal ground for the breeding and exercising of race-horses. The Arab stallions and mares which my father collected in the course of his wide travels gave rise to a breed of unexampled strength and swiftness. The Duke of Ashby-de-la-Zouche, as you of course are aware, has one great ambition. It is to own three successive Derby winners, and it is through me that he hopes to realize this ambition. His vast wealth is devoted mainly to this end. On the ground that the Derby offers an attraction to American tourists he is allowed to deduct the expenses of his stud from his income in his tax returns. He is thus able to retain that wealth which too many of his peers have lost. The Duke is not alone among my customers. Some of my best horses have gone to Virginia, others to Australia. There is no part of the world in which the royal sport is known where my horses are not famous. It is owing to them that I am able to keep up my palace and to preserve intact the sturdy human stock of our Corsican mountains.

'My life, as you will see, unlike that of General Prz, is lived on the plane of reality. I think more frequently of the dollar exchange than of Ghibelline ancestry, and I pay more attention to horse dealers than to even the most picturesque aristocratic relics. Nevertheless, when I am at home, the need to preserve the respect of the surrounding population compels me to conform to tradition. It is just possible that if you visit me in my castle you will be able to pick up some clue to the enigma which, as I see from the General's letter, is the cause of your visit to me. I shall be returning to my castle on horseback the day after tomorrow. It is a long journey, and an early start will be necessary, but if you care to present yourself at six o'clock in the morning I shall be happy to provide you with a horse on which you can accompany me to my home.'

Having by this time finished the whisky and the cigar, I thanked him somewhat effusively for his courtesy, and accepted his invitation.

V

It was still pitch dark when on the next day but one I presented myself at the door of the Count's hotel. It was a raw and gusty morning and bitterly cold, with a hint of snow in the air. But the Count seemed impervious to meteorological conditions when he

appeared upon his magnificent steed. Another, almost equally magnificent, was led to the door by his servant, and I was bidden to mount him. We set off, soon leaving the streets of the town and then, by small roads which only long experience could have enabled a man to find, we wound up and up to ever greater heights, at first through woodlands and then through open country, grass and rocks.

The Count, it appeared, was incapable of fatigue, or hunger, or thirst. Throughout a long day, with only a few moments' intermission during which we munched dry bread, ate some dates, and drank icy water from a stream, he conversed intelligently and informatively about this and that, showing a wide knowledge of the world of affairs and an acquaintance with innumerable rich men who found leisure for an interest in horses. But not one word did he utter throughout the whole of that long day on the matter which had brought me to Corsica. Gradually, in spite of the beauty of the scenery and the interest of his multi-lingual anecdotes, impatience mastered me.

'My dear Count,' I said, 'I cannot express to you how grateful I am for this chance to visit your ancestral home. But I must venture to remind you that I have come upon an errand of mercy, to save the life, or at least the reason, of a worthy friend of mine for whom I have the highest regard. You are leaving me in doubt as to whether I am serving this purpose by accompanying you on this long ride.'

'I understand your impatience,' he said, 'but you must realize that, however I adapt myself to the modern world, I cannot in these uplands accelerate the tempo which is immemorially customary. You shall, I promise you, be brought nearer to your goal before the evening ends. More than that I cannot say, for the matter does not rest with me.'

With these enigmatic words I had to be content.

We reached his castle as the sun was setting. It was built upon a steep eminence, and to every lover of architecture it was obvious that every part of it, down to the minutest detail, dated from the thirteenth century. Crossing the drawbridge we entered by a Gothic gateway into a large courtyard. Our horses were taken by a groom, and the Count led me into a vast hall, out of which, by a narrow doorway, he conducted me into the chamber that I was to occupy for the night. A huge canopied bed and heavy carved furniture of ancient design filled much of the space. Out of the window a vast prospect down innumerable winding valleys enticed the eye to a distant glimpse of sea.

'I hope,' he said, 'that you will succeed in being not too uncomfortable in this somewhat antiquated domicile.'

'I do not think that will be difficult,' said I, glancing at the blazing fire of enormous logs that spread a flickering light from the vast hearth. He informed me that dinner would be ready in an hour, and that after dinner, if all went well, something should be done to further my inquiries.

After a sumptuous dinner, he led me back to my room, and said:

'I will now introduce you to an ancient servant of this house, who, from the long years of his service here, has become a repository of all its secrets. He, I have no doubt, will be able to help you towards the solution of your problem.'

He rang the bell, and when it was answered, requested the manservant to ask the senechal to join in our conversation. After a short interval the senechal approached. I saw before me an old man, bent double with rheumatism, with white locks, and the grave air of one who has lived through much.

'This man,' said my host, 'will give you as much enlightenment as this place can afford.'

With that he withdrew.

'Old man,' said I, 'I do not know whether at your great age I may hope that your wits are what they were. I am surprised, I must confess, that the Count should refer me to you. I had fondly imagined myself worthy to deal with equals, and not only with serving men in their dotage.'

As I uttered these words a strange transformation occurred. The old man, as I had supposed him to be, suddenly lost his rheumatic appearance, drew himself up to his full height of six-foot three, tore from his head the white wig which concealed his ample coal-black hair, threw off the ancient cloak which he had been wearing, and revealed beneath it the complete costume of a Florentine noble of the period when the castle was built. Laying his hand upon his sword, he turned upon me with flashing eyes, and said:

'Young man, were you not brought here by the Count, in whose sagacity I have much confidence, I should here and now order you to be cast into the dungeons, as an impertinent upstart, unable to perceive noble blood through the disguise of a seedy cloak.'

'Sir,' I said, with all due humility, 'I must humbly beg your pardon for an error which I cannot but think was designed both by you and by the Count. If you will accept my humble excuses, I shall be happy to learn who it is in whose presence I have the honour to be.'

'Sir,' said he, 'I will accept your speech as in some degree making amends for your previous impertinence, and you shall know who I am and what I stand for. I, Sir, am the Duke of Ermocolle. The Count is my right-hand man, and obeys me in all things. But in these sad times there is need of the wisdom of the serpent. You have seen him as a business man, adapting himself to the practices of our age, blaspheming for a purpose against the noble creed by which he and I alike are inspired. I decided to present myself to you in disguise in order to form some estimate of your character and outlook. You passed the test, and I will now tell you the little that I have a right to reveal concerning the trouble which has come into the life of your unworthy professorial friend.'

In reply to these words I spoke long and eloquently about the professor and his labours, about Miss X and her youthful innocence, and about the obligation which I felt that friendship had placed upon my inadequate shoulders. He listened to me in grave silence. At the end he said:

'There is only one thing that I can do for you, and that I will do.'

He thereupon took in his hand an enormous quill pen, and on a large sheet of parchment he wrote these words: 'To Miss X. You are hereby released from a part of the oath you swore. Tell all to the bearer of this note and to Professor N. Then ACT.' To this he appended his signature in full magnificence.

'That, my friend, is all that I can do for you.'

I thanked him and bade him a ceremonial goodnight.

I slept little. The wind howled, the snow fell, the fire died down. I tossed and turned upon my pillow. When at last a few moments of uneasy slumber came to me, strange dreams wearied me even more than wakefulness. When dawn broke, a leaden oppression weighed me down. I sought the Count and acquainted him with what had passed.

'You will understand,' I said, 'that in view of the message which I bear, it is my duty to return to England with all speed.'

Thanking him once more for his hospitality I mounted the same steed upon which I had come and, accompanied by a groom whom he sent with me to help me in finding the road, I slowly picked my way through snow and sleet and tempest until I reached the shelter of Ajaccio. From there next day I returned to England.

VI

On the morning after my return I presented myself at the house of Professor N. I found him sunk in gloom, decorative art forgotten, and Miss X absent.

'Old friend,' I said, 'it is painful to see you in this sad state. I have been active on your behalf, and returned but last night from Corsica. I was not wholly successful, but I was also not wholly unsuccessful. I bear a message, not to you, but to Miss X. Whether this message will bring relief or the opposite I cannot tell. But it is my plain duty to deliver it into her hands. Can you arrange that I may see her here in your presence, for it is in your presence that the message must be delivered.'

'It shall be done,' said he.

He called to him his aged housekeeper, who with sorrowful countenance approached to know his wishes.

'I wish you,' said he, 'to find Miss X, and request her presence urgently, imperatively, and at no matter what inconvenience.'

The housekeeper departed, and he and I sat in gloomy silence. After an interval of some two hours she returned and replied that Miss X had fallen into a lethargy which had caused her to keep to her bed, but on receipt of Professor N's message some spark of doleful animation had returned to her and she had promised to be with him within a very short time. Scarcely had the housekeeper uttered this message when Miss X herself appeared, pale, distraught, with wild eyes and almost lifeless movements.

'Miss X,' I said, 'it is my duty, whether painful or not I do not yet know, to deliver to you this message from one who I believe is known to you.'

I handed over the piece of parchment. She suddenly came to life, and seized it eagerly. Her eyes ran over its few lines in a moment.

'Alas!' she said. 'This is not the reprieve for which I had hoped. It will not remove the cause of sorrow, but it does enable me to lift the veil of mystery. The story is a long one, and when I have finished it you will wish it had been longer. For when it is ended, it can be succeeded only by horror.'

The Professor, seeing that she was on the verge of collapse, administered a strong dose of brandy. He then seated us round a table and in a calm voice said:

'Proceed, Miss X.'

## VII

'When I went to Corsica,' she began, 'and how long ago that seems, as though it had been in another existence, I was happy and carefree, thinking only of pleasure, of the light enjoyments which are considered suitable to my age, and of the delight of sunshine and new scenes. Corsica from the first moment enchanted me. I acquired the practice of long rambles in the hills, and each day I extended my rambles a little further. In the golden October sunshine, the leaves of the forest shone in their many bright colours. At last I found a path that led me beyond the forest on to the bare hills.

'In all-day rambles I caught a glimpse, to my immense surprise, of a great castle on a hill-top. My curiosity was aroused. Ah! would that it had been otherwise. It was too late that day to approach any nearer to this astonishing edifice. But next day, having supplied myself with some simple sustenance, I set out early in the morning, determined, if it were possible, to discover the secret of this stately pile. Higher and higher I climbed through the sparkling autumn air. I met no human soul, and as I approached the castle it might have belonged to the Sleeping Beauty for all the signs of life that I saw about it.

'Curiosity, that fatal passion which misled our first mother, lured me on. I wandered round the battlements, seeking for a mode of ingress. For a long time my search was vain. Ah! would that it had remained so! But a malign fate willed otherwise. I found at last a little postern gate which yielded to my touch. I entered a dark abandoned out-house. When I had grown accustomed to the gloom, I saw at the far end a door standing ajar. I tip-toed to the door and glanced through. What met my gaze caused me to gasp, and I nearly emitted a cry of amazement.

'I saw before me a vast hall, in the very centre of which, at a long wooden table, were seated a number of grave men, some old, some young, some middle-aged, but all bearing upon their countenances the stamp of resolution, and the look of men born to do great deeds. "Who may these be?" I wondered. You will not be surprised to

learn that I could not bring myself to withdraw, and that standing behind that little door I listened to their words. This was my first sin on that day on which I was to sink to unimaginable depths of wickedness.

'At first I could not distinguish their words, though I could see that some portentous matter was being debated. But gradually, as my ears became attuned to their speech, I learned to follow what they were saying, and with every word my amazement grew.

' "Are we all agreed as to the day?" said the President.

' "We are," many voices replied.

' "So be it," said he. "I decree that Thursday, the 15th of November, is to be the day. And are we all agreed as to our respective tasks?" he asked.

' "We are," replied the same voices.

' "Then," he said, "I will repeat the conclusions at which we have arrived, and when I have done so, I will formally put them to the meeting and you will vote. All of us here are agreed that the human race is suffering from an appalling malady, and that the name of this malady is GOVERNMENT. We are agreed that if man is to recover the happiness that he enjoyed in the Homeric Age and which we, in this fortunate island, have in some measure retained, abolition of government is the first necessity. We are agreed also that there is only one way in which government can be abolished, and that is by abolishing governors. Twenty-one of us are here present, and we have agreed that there are twenty-one important states in the world. Each one of us on Thursday, the 15th of November, will assassinate the head of one of these twenty-one states. I, as your President, have the privilege of assigning to myself the most difficult and dangerous of these twenty-one enterprises. I allude, of course, to . . . but it is needless for me to pronounce the name. Our work, however, will not be quite complete when these twenty-one have suffered the fate that they so richly deserve. There is one other person, so ignoble, so sunk in error, so diligent in the propagation of falsehood, that he also must die. But as he is not of so exalted a status as these other twenty-one victims, I appoint my squire to effect his demise. You will all realize that I speak of Professor N, who has had the temerity to maintain in many learned journals and in a vast work which, as our secret service has informed us, is nearing completion, that it was from Lithuania, and not, as all of us know, from Corsica, that pre-Celtic decorative art spread over Europe. He also shall die."

'At this point,' Miss X continued, amid sobs, 'I could contain myself no longer. The thought that my benevolent employer was to die so soon afflicted me profoundly, and I gave an involuntary cry. All heads looked towards the door. The henchman to whom the extermination of Professor N had been assigned was ordered to investigate. Before I could escape he seized me and led me before the twenty-one. The President bent stern eyes upon me and frowned heavily.

' "Who are you," said he, "that has so rashly, so impiously, intruded upon our secret councils? What has led you to eavesdrop upon the most momentous decision that any body of men has ever arrived at? Can you offer any reason whatever why you should not, here and now, die the death which your temerity has so richly merited?" '

At this point hesitation overcame Miss X, and she was scarcely able to continue her account of the momentous interview in the castle. At length she pulled herself together and resumed the narrative.

'I come now,' she said, 'to the most painful part of my story. It is a merciful dispensation of Providence that the future is concealed from our gaze. Little did my mother think, as she lay exhausted, listening to my first cry, that it was to this that her new-born daughter was destined. Little did I think as I entered the Secretarial College that it was to lead to this. Little did I dream that Pitman's was but the gateway to the gallows. But I must not waste time in vain repining. What is done is done, and it is my duty to relate the plain unvarnished tale without the trimmings of futile remorse.

'As the President spoke to me of swift death, I glimpsed the pleasant sunshine without. I thought of the carefree years of my youth. I thought of the promise of happiness which but that very morning had accompanied me as I climbed the lonely hills. Visions of summer rain and winter firesides, of spring in meadows and autumn in the beech woods haunted my imagination. I thought of the golden years of innocent childhood, fled never to return. And I thought fleetingly and shyly of one in whose eyes I fancied that I had seen the light of love. All this in a moment passed through my mind. "Life," I thought, "is sweet. I am but young, and the best of life is still before me. Am I to be cut off thus, before I have known the joys, and the sorrows too, which make the warp and woof of human life? No," I thought, "this is too much. If there yet remains a means by which I may prolong my life I will seize it, even though it be at the price of dishonour." When Satan had led me to this dreadful resolve I answered with such calmness as I could command: "Oh, reverend Sir, I have been but an unwitting and unintentional offender. No thought of evil was in my mind as I strayed through that fatal door. If you will but spare my life I will do your will, whatever it may be. Have mercy, I pray you. You cannot wish that one so young and fair should perish prematurely. Let me but know your will and I will obey." Although he still looked down upon me with no friendly eye, I fancied I saw some slight sign of relenting. He turned to the other twenty, and said:

"What is your will? Shall we execute justice, or shall we submit her to the ordeal? I will put it to the vote." Ten voted for justice, ten for the ordeal. "The casting vote is mine," he said. "I vote for the ordeal."

'Then turning again to me, he continued: "You may live, but on certain terms. What these terms are I will now explain to you. First of all you must swear a great oath—never to reveal by word or deed, by any hint or by any turn of demeanour, what you have learned in this hall. The oath which you must fulfil I will now tell you, and you must repeat the words after me: I SWEAR BY ZOROASTER AND THE BEARD OF THE PROPHET, BY URIENS, PAYMON, EGYN AND AMAYMON, BY MARBUEL, ACIEL, BARBIEL, MEPHISTOPHIEL AND APADIEL, BY DIRACHIEL, AMNODIEL, AMUDIEL, TAGRIEL, GELIEL AND REQUIEL, AND BY ALL THE FOUL SPIRITS OF HELL, THAT I WILL NEVER REVEAL OR IN ANY MANNER CAUSE TO BE KNOWN ANY SLIGHTEST HINT OF WHAT I HAVE SEEN AND HEARD IN THIS HALL." When I had solemnly repeated this oath, he explained to me that this was but the first part of the ordeal, and that perhaps I might not have grasped its full immensity. Each of the infernal names that I had invoked possessed its own separate power of torture. By the magician's power invested in himself he was able to control the actions of these demons. If I infringed the oath, each separate one would, through all eternity, inflict upon me the separate torture of which he was master. But that, he said, was but the smallest part of my punishment.

' "I come now," said he, "to graver matters."

'Turning to the henchman, he said: "The goblet, please."

'The henchman, who knew the ritual, presented the goblet to the President.

' "This," he said, turning again to me, "is a goblet of bull's blood. You must drink every drop, without taking breath while you drink. If you fail to do so, you will instantly become a cow, and be pursued forever by the ghost of the bull whose blood you will have failed to drink in due manner." I took the goblet from him, drew a long breath, closed my eyes, and swallowed the noxious draught.

' "Two-thirds of the ordeal," he said, " are now fulfilled. The last part is slightly more inconvenient. We have decreed, as you are unfortunately aware, that on the 15th prox., twenty-one heads of state shall die. We decided also that the glory of our nation demands the death of Professor N. But we felt that there would be a lack of symmetry if one of us were to undertake this just execution. Before we discovered your presence, we delegated this task to my henchman. But your arrival, while in many ways inopportune, has in one respect provided us with an opportunity for neatness which it would be unwise and inartistic to neglect. You, and not my henchman, shall carry out this execution. And this to do you shall swear by the same oath by which you swore secrecy."

' "Oh Sir!" I said, "do not put upon me this terrible burden. You know much, but I doubt whether you know that it has been both my duty and my pleasure to assist Professor N in his researches. I have had nothing but kindness from him. It may be that his views on decorative art are not all that you could wish. Can you not permit me to continue serving him as before, and gradually I could wean him from his errors. I am not without influence upon the course of his thoughts. Several years of close association have shown me ways of guiding his inclinations in this direction or that, and I am persuaded that if you will but grant me time I can bring him round to your opinions on the function of Corsica in pre-Celtic decorative art. To slay this good old man, whom I have regarded as a friend and who has hitherto, and not unjustly, regarded me in not unlike manner, would be almost as terrible as the pursuit of the many fiends whom you have caused me to invoke. Indeed, I doubt whether life is worth purchasing at such a price."

' "Nay, my good maiden," said he, "I fear you are still indulging in illusions. The oath you have already taken was a sinful and blasphemous oath, and has put you forever in the power of the fiends, unless I, by my magic art, choose to restrain them. You cannot escape now. You must do my will or suffer." I wept, I implored him, I knelt and clasped his knees. "Have mercy," I said, "have mercy." But he remained unmoved. "I have spoken," he said. "If you do not wish to suffer forever the fifteen separate kinds

THE CORSICAN ORDEAL OF MISS X 83

of torment that will be inflicted by each of the fifteen fiends you have invoked, you must repeat after me, using the same dread names, the oath that on the 15th prox. you will cause the death of Professor N."

'Alas! dear Professor. It is impossible that you should pardon me, but in my weakness I swore this second oath. The 15th, no longer prox. but inst., is rapidly approaching, and I see not how I am to escape, when that day comes, the dread consequences of my frightful oath. As soon as I got away from that dreadful castle, remorse seized me and has gnawed at my vitals ever since. Gladly would I suffer the fifteen diverse torments of the fifteen fiends, could I but persuade myself that in doing so I should be fulfilling the behests of duty. But I have sworn, and honour demands that I should fulfil my oath. Which is the greater sin, to murder the good man whom I revere, or to be false to the dictates of honour? I know not. But you, dear Professor, you who are so wise, you, I am sure, can resolve my doubts, and show me the clear path of duty.'

VIII

The Professor, as her narrative advanced towards its climax, somewhat surprisingly recovered cheerfulness and calm. With a kindly smile, with folded hands and a completely peaceful demeanour, he replied to her query.

'My dear young lady,' he said, 'nothing, nothing on earth, should be allowed to override the dictates of honour. If it lies in your power you must fulfil your oath. My work is completed, and my remaining years, if any, could have little importance. I should therefore tell you in the most emphatic manner that it is your duty to fulfil your oath if it is in any way possible. I should regret, however, I might even say I should regret deeply, that as a consequence of your sense of honour you should end your life upon the gallows. There is one thing, and one thing only, which can absolve you from your oath, and that is physical impossibility. You cannot kill a dead man.'

So saying, he put his thumb and forefinger into his waistcoat pocket and with a lightning gesture conveyed them to his mouth. In an instant he was dead.

'Oh, my dear master,' cried Miss X, throwing herself upon his lifeless corpse, 'how can I bear the light of day now that you have sacrificed your life for mine? How can I endure the shame that every hour of sunshine and every moment of seeming happiness will generate in my soul? Nay, not another moment can I endure this agony.'

With these words, she found the same pocket, imitated his gesture, and expired.

'I have not lived in vain,' said I, 'for I have witnessed two noble deaths.' But then I remembered that my task was not done, since the world's unworthy rulers must, I supposed, be saved from extinction. Reluctantly I bent my footsteps towards Scotland Yard.

# THE INFRA-REDIOSCOPE

I

Lady Millicent Pinturque, known to her friends as the lovely Millicent, was sitting alone in her armchair in her luxurious boudoir. All the chairs and sofas were soft; the electric light was softly shaded; beside her, on a small table, stood what appeared to be a large doll with voluminous skirts. The walls were covered with water colours, all signed 'Millicent,' representing romantic scenes in the Alps and the Italian shores of the Mediterranean, in the islands of Greece, and in Teneriffe. Another water colour was in her hands, and she was scrutinizing it with minute care. At last she reached out her hand to the doll, and touched a button. The doll opened in the middle, and revealed a telephone in its entrails. She lifted the receiver. Her movements, although they showed what was evidently an habitual grace, displayed a certain tenseness of manner, suggesting an important decision just arrived at. She called a number, and when it had been obtained she said: 'I wish to speak with Sir Bulbus.'

Sir Bulbus Frutiger was known to all the world as the editor of the *Daily Lightning*, and as one of the great powers in our land, no matter what party might be nominally in office. He was protected from the public by a secretary and six secretary's secretaries. Few ventured to call him on the telephone, and of these few only an infinitesimal proportion reached him. His lucubrations were too important to be interrupted. It was his mission to preserve an imperturbable calm, while developing schemes for destroying the calm of all his readers. But in spite of this wall of protection, he answered instantly to the call of Lady Millicent.

'Yes, Lady Millicent?' he said.

'All is ready,' she answered, and replaced the receiver.

II

Much preparation had preceded these brief words. The lovely Millicent's husband, Sir Theophilus Pinturque, was one of the leaders in the world of finance, an immensely rich man, but not, though this grieved him, without rivals in the world that he wished to dominate. There were still men who could meet him on equal terms and who, in a financial contest, had reasonable chances of victory. His character was Napoleonic, and he sought for means by which his superiority could become unchallenged and unquestionable. He recognized that the power of finance was not the only great power in the modern world. There are, he reflected, three others: one is the power of the Press; one is the power of advertising; and one, too often underestimated by men in his profession, is the power of science. He decided that victory would require a combination of these four powers, and with this end in view, he formed a secret committee of four.

He himself was the chairman. Next in power and dignity was Sir Bulbus Frutiger, who had a slogan: 'Give the public what it wants.' This slogan governed all his vast chain of newspapers. The third member of the syndicate was Sir Publius Harper, who controlled the advertising world. Those who, in compelled, though temporary, idleness went up and down escalators, imagined that the men whose advertisements they read, because they had nothing else to do, were rivals. This was a mistake. All the advertisements came to a central pool, and in that central pool their distribution was decided by Sir Publius Harper. If he wished your dentrifice to be known, it would be known; if he wished it ignored, it would be ignored, however excellent. It rested with him to make or mar the fortunes of those who were unwise enough to produce consumable commodities—instead of recommending them. Sir Publius had a certain kindly contempt for Sir Bulbus. He thought Sir Bulbus's slogan too submissive altogether. His slogan was: 'Make the public want what you give it.' In this he was amazingly successful. Wines of unspeakable nastiness sold in vast numbers because, when he told the public that they were delicious, the public had not the courage to doubt his word. Seaside resorts where hotels were filthy, the lodgings dingy, and the sea, except at extreme high tide, a sea of mud, acquired through the activities of Sir Publius a reputation for ozone, stormy seas, and invigorating Atlantic breezes. Political parties at General Elections made use of the inventiveness of his employees, which was at the service of all (except Communists) who could afford his prices. No sensible man who knew the world would dream of launching a campaign without the support of Sir Publius.

Sir Bulbus and Sir Publius, though frequently joined in their public campaigns, were in appearance very different from each other. Both were *bons viveurs,* but while Sir Bulbus looked the part, having a considerable corporation and a cheerful, eupeptic appearance, Sir Publius was lean and ascetic-looking. Anybody who did not know who he was would imagine him an earnest seeker after some mystic vision. Never could his portrait be used to advertise any article of food or drink. Nevertheless, when, as not infrequently occurred, the two men dined together, to plan a new conquest or a change of policy, they agreed remarkably with each other. Each understood the workings of the other's mind; each respected the other's ambitions; each felt the need of the other to complete his designs. Sir Publius would point out how much Sir

Bulbus owed to the picture which appeared on every hoarding of the moron who does not read the *Daily Lightning*, pointed at with contempt by a well-dressed crowd of handsome men and lovely women, each supplied with his or her copy of that great newspaper. And Sir Bulbus would retort: 'Yes, but where would you be, but for my great campaign to secure control of the Canadian forests? Where would you be without paper, and where would you get the paper, but for the masterly policy which I have pursued in that great Transatlantic Dominion?' Such friendly quips would occupy them until the dessert; after that, both would become serious, and their co-operation would be intense and creative.

Pendrake Markle, the fourth member of the secret syndicate, was somewhat different from the other three. Sir Bulbus and Sir Publius had had some doubts as to his admission, but their doubts had been overruled by Sir Theophilus. Their doubts were not unreasonable. In the first place, unlike the other three, he had not been honoured with a knighthood. There were, however, even graver objections to him. Nobody denied that he was brilliant, but solid men suspected that he was unsound. His was not the sort of name that would be put on a prospectus to tempt country investors. Sir Theophilus, however, insisted upon including him, because of his extreme fertility in unorthodox invention, and also because, unlike some other men of science, he was not hampered by an undue scrupulosity.

He had a grudge against the human race, which was intelligible to those who knew his history. His father was a Nonconformist minister of the most exemplary piety, who used to explain to him when he was a little boy how right it was of Elisha to curse the children who, as a result of his curse, were torn to pieces by she-bears. In all ways his father was a relic of a bygone age. Respect for the Sabbath, and a belief in the literal inspiration of every word of the Old and New Testaments, dominated all his converse in the home. The boy, already intelligent, once ventured in a rash moment to ask his father whether it was impossible to be a good Christian if one did not believe that the hare chews the cud. His father thrashed him so unmercifully that he could not sit down for a week.

In spite of this careful upbringing, he refused to gratify the parental desire that he should become himself a Nonconformist minister. By means of scholarships he managed to work his way through the university, where he obtained the highest honours. His first piece of research was stolen from him by his professor, who was awarded a Royal Society Medal on the strength of it. When he attempted to make his grievance known, no one believed him, and he was thought to be an ill-conditioned boor. As a result of this experience and of the suspicion with which his protests caused him to be regarded, he became a cynic and a misanthropist. He took care, however, henceforth, that no one should steal his inventions or discoveries. There were nasty stories, never substantiated, of shady dealings in regard to patents. The stories varied, and no one knew what foundation they had in fact. However that may be, he acquired at last enough money to make for his own use a private laboratory, to which no possible rivals were allowed access. Gradually his work began to win reluctant recognition. At last the Government approached him with a request that he should devote his talents to improving bacteriological warfare. He refused this request on a ground which was universally considered exceedingly strange, namely that he knew nothing about bacteriology. It was suspected, however, that his real reason was a hatred of all the forces of organized society, from the Prime Minister to the humblest policeman on his beat.

Although everybody in the scientific world disliked him, very few dared to attack him, because of his unscrupulous skill in controversy, which succeeded almost always in making his adversary look foolish. There was only one thing in all the world that he loved, and that was his private laboratory. Unfortunately, its equipment had run him into enormous expense and he was in imminent danger of having to dispose of it to settle his debts. It was while this danger hung over him that he was approached by Sir Theophilus, who offered to save him from disaster in return for his help as the fourth member of the secret syndicate.

At the first meeting of the syndicate, Sir Theophilus explained what he had in mind, and asked for suggestions as to the realization of his hopes. It should be possible, he said, for the four of them in collaboration to achieve complete domination of the world—not only of this or that part of the world, not only of Western Europe, or of Western Europe and America, but equally of the world on the other side of the Iron Curtain. If they used their skill and their opportunities wisely, nothing should be able to resist them.

'All that is wanted,' so he said in his opening address, 'is a really fruitful idea. The supplying of ideas shall be the business of Markle. Given a good idea, I will finance it, Harper will advertise it, and Frutiger will rouse to frenzy the passions of the public against those who oppose it. It is possible that Markle may require a little time to invent the sort of idea which the rest of us would think it worth while to promote. I therefore propose that this meeting do adjourn for a week, at the end of which time, I am convinced, science will be prepared to vindicate its position as one of the four forces dominating our society.'

With this, after a bow to Mr. Markle, he dismissed the meeting.

When the syndicate met again a week later, Sir Theophilus, smiling at Mr. Markle, remarked: 'Well, Markle, and what has science to say?' Markle cleared his throat and entered upon a speech:

'Sir Theophilus, Sir Bulbus and Sir Publius,' he began, 'throughout the past week I have given my best thought—and my best thought, I assure you, is very good—to the concoction of such a scheme as was adumbrated at our last meeting. Various notions occurred to me, only to be rejected. The public has been inundated with horrors connected with nuclear energy, and I decided very quickly that this whole subject has now become hackneyed. Moreover, it is a matter as to which Governments are on the alert, and anything that we might attempt in this direction would probably meet with official opposition. I thought next of what could be done by means of bacteriology. It might be possible, so I thought, to give hydrophobia to all the Heads of State. But it was not quite clear how we should profit by this, and there was always a risk that one of them might bite one of us before his disease was diagnosed. Then, of course, there was the scheme for creating a satellite of the earth which should complete its revolution once every three days, with a clockwork mechanism timed to fire at the Kremlin every time it passed that way. This, however, is a project for Governments. We should be above the battle. It is not for us to take sides in the controversies between East and West. It is for us to ensure that, whatever happens, we shall be supreme. I therefore rejected all schemes which involve an abandonment of neutrality.

'I have a scheme to propose to you which I think is not open to any of the objections to the other schemes. The public has heard much in recent years about infra-red photography. It is as ignorant on this subject as on every other, and I see no reason why we should not exploit its ignorance. I propose that we invent a machine to be called the "infra-redioscope," which (so we shall assure the public) will photograph by means of infra-red rays objects not otherwise perceptible. It shall be a very delicate machine, capable of getting out of order if carelessly handled. We shall see to it that this happens whenever the machine is in the possession of persons whom we cannot control. What it is to see we shall determine, and I think that, by our united efforts, we can persuade the world that it really sees whatever we shall decide that it makes visible. If you adopt my scheme, I will undertake to devise the machine, but as to how it is to be utilized, that, I think, is a matter for Sir Bulbus and Sir Publius.'

Both these gentlemen had listened with attention to the suggestion of Pendrake Markle. Both of them seized upon his ideas with enthusiasm, seeing great opportunities for the exploitation of their respective skills.

'I know,' said Sir Bulbus, 'what it is that the machine should reveal. It shall reveal a secret invasion from Mars, an invasion of horrible creatures, whose invisible army, but for our machine, would be certain of victory. I shall, in all my newspapers, rouse the public to a consciousness of their peril. Millions of them will buy the machine. Sir Theophilus will make the greatest fortune ever possessed by a single man. My newspapers will outsell all others and will be, before long, the only newspapers of the world. Nor will my friend Publius be less important in this campaign.

He will cover every hoarding with pictures of the dreadful creatures and a caption beneath—"Do you wish to be dispossessed by THIS?" And in vast letters he will put notices along all the main roads, in all stations of the country, and wherever the public has leisure to see such things, and the notices will say: "Men of earth, now is the hour of decision. Rise in your millions. Be not appalled by the cosmic danger. Courage shall yet triumph, as it has done ever since the days of Adam. Buy an infra-redioscope and be prepared!" '

At this point Sir Theophilus intervened.

'The scheme is good,' he said. 'It requires only one thing, and that is that the picture of the Martian should be sufficiently horrible and terrifying. You all know Lady Millicent, but you know her perhaps only in her gentler aspects. I, as her husband, have been privileged to become aware of regions in her imagination which are concealed from most people. She is, as you know, skilled in water colours. Let her make a water-colour picture of the Martian, and let photographs of her picture form the basis of our campaign.'

The others at first looked a little doubtful. Lady Millicent as they had seen her was soft, perhaps a trifle silly, not the sort of person whom they had imagined as taking part in so grim a campaign. After some debate it was decided to allow her to make the attempt, and if her picture was sufficiently dreadful to satisfy Mr. Markle, Sir Bulbus should then be informed that all was in readiness for the launching of the campaign.

Sir Theophilus, on returning home from this momentous meeting, set to work to explain to the lovely Millicent what it was that he wanted. He did not enlarge upon the general aspects of his campaign, for it was a principle with him that one should not take women into one's confidence. He told her merely that he wished for pictures of terrifying imaginary creatures, for which he had a business use which she would find it difficult to understand.

Lady Millicent, who was very much younger than Sir Theophilus, belonged to a good county family now fallen upon evil days. Her father, an impoverished earl, was the owner of an exquisite Elizabethan mansion, which he loved with a devotion inherited from all the generations that had inhabited it. It had seemed

inevitable that he should sell this ancestral mansion to some rich Argentinian, and the prospect was slowly breaking his heart. His daughter adored him, and decided to use her staggering beauty to enable him to end his days in peace. Almost all men adored her at sight. Sir Theophilus was the richest of her adorers and so she chose him, exacting as her price a sufficient settlement upon her father to free him from all financial anxiety. She did not dislike Sir Theophilus, who adored her and gratified her every whim, but she did not love him—indeed, no one, up to this moment, had ever touched her heart. She felt it her duty, in return for all he gave her, to obey him whenever possible.

His request for a water colour of a monster seemed to her a little odd, but she was accustomed to actions on his part to which she had no clue, nor had she ever any desire to understand his business schemes. She therefore duly set to work. He did go so far as to tell her that the picture was wanted for the purpose of showing what could be seen by means of a new instrument to be called the 'infra-redioscope.' After several attempts which did not satisfy her, she produced a picture of a creature with a body somewhat resembling that of a beetle, but six feet long, with seven hairy legs, with a human face, completely bald head, staring eyes, and a fixed grin. She made indeed two pictures. In the first, a man is looking through an infra-redioscope and seeing this creature. In the second, the man, in terror, has dropped the instrument. The monster, seeing that it is observed, has stood upright on its seventh leg, and is entwining the other six in hairy embrace round the asphyxiated man. These two pictures, at the orders of Sir Theophilus, she showed to Mr. Markle. Mr. Markle accepted them as adequate, and it was after his departure that she telephoned the fateful words to Sir Bulbus.

III

As soon as Sir Bulbus received this message, the vast apparatus controlled by the syndicate was set in motion. Sir Theophilus caused innumerable workshops throughout the world to manufacture the infra-redioscope, a simple machine, containing a lot of wheels that made whirring noises, but not in fact enabling anyone to see anything. Sir Bulbus filled his newspapers with articles on the wonders of science, all of them with a 'slant' towards the infrared. Some of these contained genuine information by reputable men of science; others were more imaginative. Sir Publius had bills posted everywhere: 'The infra-redioscope is coming! See the world's invisible marvels!' or 'What is the infra-redioscope? The Harper newspapers will tell you. Do not miss this chance of strange knowledge!'

As soon as sufficient numbers of infra-redioscopes had been manufactured, Lady Millicent let it be known that by means of one of these instruments she had observed the horror crawling upon her bedroom floor. She was interviewed naturally by all the newspapers under the control of Sir Bulbus, but the matter was of such dramatic interest that other newspapers were compelled to follow suit. Under her husband's instructions, she uttered in broken and apparently terrified sentences exactly the sentiments that were required by the scheme of the syndicate. At the same time infra-redioscopes were given to various leaders of opinion whom Sir Theophilus, by means of his secret service, knew to be in financial difficulties. Each of them was offered a thousand pounds if he would say that he had seen one of the awful creatures. Lady Millicent's two pictures were reproduced everywhere through the advertising agency of Sir Publius, with the legend: 'Do not drop your infra-redioscope. It protects as well as reveals.'

There was, of course, an instant sale of many thousands of infra-redioscopes and a world-wide wave of horror. Pendrake Markle invented a new instrument to be found only in his private laboratory. This new instrument proved that the creatures came from Mars. Other men of science grew envious of the enormous fame which accrued to Markle, and one of the more venturesome of these would-be rivals invented a machine that read the thoughts of the creatures. By means of this machine he professed to have discovered that they were the advance guard of a Martian campaign to exterminate the human race.

Just at first the earlier purchasers of infra-redioscopes had complained that they saw nothing through these instruments, but naturally their remarks were not printed in any of the newspapers controlled by Sir Bulbus, and very soon the universal panic reached such dimensions that any person claiming to have failed to detect the presence of Martians was assumed to be a traitor and pro-Martian. After some thousands of persons had been lynched, the rest found it prudent to hold their tongues, except for a very few who were interned. There was now such a wave of horror that many people who had hitherto been considered harmless incurred the gravest suspicion. Any person who unguardedly praised the appearance of the planet Mars in the night sky was instantly suspect. All astronomers who had made a special study of Mars were interned. Those among them who had maintained that there is no life on Mars were sentenced to long terms of imprisonment.

There were, however, some groups who, throughout the early stages of the panic, remained friends of Mars. The Emperor of Abyssinia announced that a careful study of the picture showed the Martian to resemble closely the Lion of Judah, and to be therefore obviously good and not bad. The Tibetans said that from a study of ancient books they had concluded that the Martian was a Boddhisatva, come to liberate them from the yoke of the infidel Chinese. Peruvian Indians revived sun-worship, and pointed out that since Mars shines by reflected sunlight, Mars too is to be adored. When it was remarked that the Martians might cause carnage, they replied that sun-worship had always involved human sacrifice, and that therefore the truly devout would not repine. The anarchists argued that Martians would dissolve all government and would therefore bring the millennium. The pacifists said that they should be met with love, and that if the love were sufficiently great, it would take the grin off their faces.

For a short time these various groups, wherever they existed in sufficient numbers, remained unmolested. But their respite ceased when the Communist world was brought into the anti-Martian campaign. This was achieved by the syndicate with some skill. They approached first certain Western men of science known to be friendly to the Soviet Government. They told these men frankly how the campaign had been engineered. They pointed out that fear of the Martians could be made the basis of reconciliation between East and West. They also succeeded in persuading the fellow-travelling scientists that an East-West war could well result in the defeat of the East, and that therefore whatever would prevent a third world war should be favoured by the Communists. They pointed out further that if terror of the Martians was to effect a reconciliation between East and West, it was necessary that all the governments, Eastern as well as Western, should believe in the Martian invasion. The fellow-travelling scientists, after listening to these arguments, found themselves reluctantly compelled to agree. For were they not realists? And was not this realism, as stark as realism could be? And was not this perhaps the very synthesis that dialectical materialism demanded? They therefore agreed that they would not reveal to the Soviet Government the fact that the whole thing was a hoax. For its own sake they would allow it to believe this plot, inaugurated by vile capitalists for vile capitalist ends, but incidentally and accidentally furthering the interests of mankind, and giving a chance that when, in due course, the deception was unmasked a general reaction would sweep the whole world into the arms of Moscow. Convinced by this reasoning, they represented to Moscow the imminent danger of the destruction of the human race, and pointed out that there was no reason to believe the Martians to be Communists. On the basis of their representations, Moscow, after some hesitation, decided to join with the West in the anti-Martian campaign.

From this moment the Abyssinians, the Tibetans, the Peruvians, the anarchists, and the pacifists received short shrift. Some were killed, some were set to forced labour, some recanted, and in a very short time there was no longer any explicit opposition anywhere in the world to the great anti-Martian campaign.

Fear, however, could not be confined to fear of the Martians. There was still fear of traitors in their midst. A great meeting of the United Nations was summoned to organize propaganda and publicity. It was felt that a word was needed to represent the inhabitants of earth as opposed to the inhabitants of other planets. 'Earthy' obviously would not do. 'Earthly' was inadequate because the usual alternative was 'heavenly.' 'Terrestrial' would not do because the usual alternative was 'celestial.' At last, after much eloquence, in which the South Americans especially distinguished themselves, the word 'Tellurian' was adopted. The United Nations then appointed a committee against un-Tellurian activities, which established a political reign of terror throughout the whole world. It was also decided that the United Nations should be in permanent session, so long as the crisis lasted, under a permanent head. A President was chosen from among the elder statesmen, a man of immense dignity and vast experience, no longer embroiled in party warfare, and prepared by two world wars for the even more terrible war that now seemed imminent. He rose to the occasion, and in his opening address said:

'Friends, Fellow inhabitants of Earth, Tellurians, united as never before, I address you on this solemn occasion, not as heretofore in the cause of world peace, but in an even greater cause—an even greater cause—the cause of the preservation of this our human existence with all its human values, with all its joys and sorrows, all its hopes and all its fears, the preservation, I say, of this our human life from a foul assault wafted across the ether by we know not what foul and dreadful means, revealed to us, I am happy to say, by the amazing skill of our men of science, who have shown us what by infra-rediation can be discovered, and have made visible to us the strange, repellent and horrible beasts which crawl upon our floors unseen save by these marvellous instruments, which crawl, I say, nay, which infect us, which pollute our very thoughts, which would destroy within us the very fibre of our moral being, which would reduce us, I say, not to the level of beasts—for beasts are, after all, Tellurians—nay, to the level of Martians—and can I say anything worse? No lower term, no greater word of infamy exists in the languages of this Earth that we all love. I call upon you, I call upon you, my brethren, to stand shoulder to shoulder in the great fight, the fight to preserve our earthly values against this insidious and degrading invasion of monsters, alien monsters, monsters who, we can only say, should go back where they came from.'

With this he sat down. And the applause was such that for five several minutes nothing else could be heard. The next speaker was the Representative of the United States.

'Fellow citizens of Earth,' he began, 'those who have had the misfortune to be compelled by their public duties to study that abominable planet against whose evil machinations we are here embattled, are aware that its surface is scarred by strange straight marks, known among astronomers as canals. These marks, as must be evident to every student of economic activity, can only be the product of totalitarianism. We have therefore a right, the right of the highest scientific authority, to believe that these invaders threaten not only us in our personal and private being, but also that way of life which was established by our ancestors nearly two hundred years ago, and which, until the present danger, produced unity—unity apparently threatened by a certain Power, which, at the present moment it would be injudicious to name. It may be that man represents but a passing phase in the evolution of the life

# THE INFRA-REDIOSCOPE

of the cosmos, but there is one law which the cosmos will always obey, one divine law, the law of eternal progress. This law, fellow citizens of Earth, this law is safeguarded by free enterprise, the immortal heritage which the West has brought to man. Free enterprise must have long since ceased in that red planet which now menaces us, for the canals which we see are not a thing of yesterday. Not only in the name of Man, but in the name of free enterprise, I call upon this Assembly to give of its best, to give till it hurts, without stint, without thought of self. It is with confident hope that I make this appeal to all the other nations here assembled.'

It was not to be left to the West alone to sound the note of unity. No sooner had the Representative of the United States sat down than he was succeeded by Mr. Growlovsky, the Representative of the Soviet Union.

'The hour is come,' he said, 'to fight, not to speak. Were I to speak, there are things which I could controvert in the speech which we have just heard. Astronomy is Russian. Some few sparse students of the subject have existed in other countries, but Soviet erudition has shown how shallow and imitative their theories have been. Of these we have had an example in what has just been said about the canals in that infamous planet which I disdain to name. The great astronomer Lukupsky has shown conclusively that it was private enterprise that produced the canals, and that it was competition that stimulated their duplication. But this is not the hour for such reflections. This is the hour for action, and when the assault has been repelled, it will be found that the world has become one, and that in the throes of battle, totalitarianism has become, willy-nilly, universal.'

Some fears were felt at this point that the new-found unity of the Great Powers might not survive the strain of public debate. India, Paraguay, and Iceland poured oil upon the troubled waters, and at last the soothing words of the Republic of Andorra enabled the delegates to separate with that glow of harmony that resulted from ignorance of each other's sentiments. Before separating, the Assembly decreed world peace and an amalgamation of the armed forces of the planet. It was hoped that the main assault of the Martians might be delayed until this amalgamation was complete. But meanwhile, in spite of all preparations, in spite of harmony, in spite of pretended confidence, fear lurked in every heart—except those of the syndicate and its coadjutors.

IV

Throughout this period of excited panic, however, there were some who, though prudence kept them silent, had their doubts about the whole matter. Members of Governments knew that they themselves had never seen the Martian monster, and their private secretaries knew that *they* had never seen them, but while the terror was at its height, neither dared to confess this, since avowed scepticism involved a fall from power and perhaps even a lynching. The business rivals of Sir Theophilus, Sir Bulbus, and Sir Publius naturally were envious of the immense success which these men were achieving, and wished, if it were in any way possible, to find some means of bringing them down. The *Daily Thunder* had been almost as great a power as the *Daily Lightning*, but while the campaign was at its height, the *Daily Thunder* was inaudible. Its editor gnashed his teeth, but, as a prudent man, he bided his time, knowing that a popular frenzy, while it lasts, cannot be opposed with profit. The scientists, who had always disliked and distrusted Pendrake Markle, were naturally indignant to see him treated as though he were the greatest scientist of all time. Many of them had taken the infra-redioscope to pieces and had seen that it was a fraud, but since they valued their own skins, they thought it wise to be silent.

Among them all, only one young man was indifferent to the claims of prudence. This young man was Thomas Shovelpenny, who was still viewed in many English quarters with suspicion because his grandfather had been a German named Schimmelpfennig and had changed his name during the first world war. Thomas Shovelpenny was a quiet student, totally unaccustomed to great affairs, ignorant of politics and economics alike, and skilled only in physics. He was too poor to buy an infra-redioscope and therefore was unable to make for himself the discovery of its fraudulent character. Those who had made this discovery kept their knowledge secret and did not whisper it even in moments of vinous conviviality. But Thomas Shovelpenny could not but observe strange discrepancies in the reported observations, and these discrepancies bred in him purely scientific doubts, though in his innocence he was totally at a loss to imagine what purpose could be served by inventing such myths.

Though himself a man of exemplary and abstemious conduct, he had a friend whom he valued for his penetration and his insight, in spite of habits by no means such as a well-behaved student could approve of. This friend, whose name was Verity Hogg-Paucus, was almost always intoxicated, and scarcely to be met with except in public houses. It was supposed that he must sleep somewhere, but he did not allow anyone to know the truth, which was that he had a single bed-room in one of the worst slums of London. He had brilliant talents as a journalist, and when his money gave out, the enforced sobriety would lead him to write articles of such mordant wit that the journals which liked that sort of thing could not refuse to publish them. The better-class journals, of course, were closed to him, since he would make no concessions to humbug. He knew all the underworld of politics, but did not know how to make his knowledge advantageous to himself. He had had many jobs, but had lost them all through allowing his chiefs to know that he had discovered shady secrets which the chiefs wished to keep concealed. Whether from imprudence or from a remnant of moral feeling, he had never made a penny by blackmailing the objects of his unpleasant knowledge. Instead of using his knowledge to his own advantage, he would let it trickle out of him in bibulous loquacity while drinking with any casual acquaintance in some unfashionable bar.

Shovelpenny consulted him in his perplexity.

'It seems to me,' he said, 'that this whole business must be fraudulent, and yet I cannot imagine either how the fraud is worked or what purpose it can serve. Perhaps you, with your great knowledge of what men wish to keep secret, will be able to help me to understand what is happening.'

Hogg-Paucus, who had watched cynically the growth of public hysteria and Sir Theophilus's fortune, was delighted.

'You,' he said, 'are the very man I want. I have no doubt that the whole thing is bogus, but remember that it is dangerous to say so. Perhaps together, you, with your knowledge of science, and I, with my knowledge of politics, we shall be able to unravel the mystery. But since it is dangerous to talk, and since I am garrulous in my cups, it will be necessary for you to keep me locked up in your rooms, and if you supply me with sufficient liquor, I shall be able to endure the temporary imprisonment without excessive discomfort.'

Shovelpenny liked the proposal, but his purse was limited, and he did not see how he could hope to keep Hogg-Paucus in drink throughout a period which might not be short. Hogg-Paucus, however, who had not always been so low in the social scale, had known Lady Millicent when both were children, and wrote a flamboyant article about her virtues and charms at the age of ten, which he sold for a large sum to a fashion magazine. This, it was thought, together with Shovelpenny's salary as a school teacher, would, with care and economy, supply the necessary amount of drink for the necessary period of time.

Hogg-Paucus thereupon set to work on a systematic investigation. It was obvious that the campaign had begun from the *Daily Lightning*. Hogg-Paucus, who knew everything in the way of personal gossip, was aware that the *Daily Lightning* was intimately connected with Sir Theophilus. It was common knowledge that Lady Millicent had been the first to see a Martian, and that Markle was mainly instrumental in the scientific part of the proceedings. A vague outline of what must have happened formed itself in the fertile mind of Hogg-Paucus, but it seemed impossible to arrive at anything more definite unless some one of those who knew could be induced to speak. Hogg-Paucus advised Shovelpenny to request an interview with Lady Millicent, as being the originator of the first photograph, and therefore clearly concerned in the very beginning of the whole matter. Shovelpenny only half believed the various cynical hypotheses that his friend produced, but his scientific mind showed him that the best way to begin an investigation would be an interview with Lady Millicent, as Hogg-Paucus advised. He therefore wrote her a careful letter, saying that he wished to see her on a matter of importance. Somewhat to his surprise, she agreed, and made an appointment. He brushed his hair and his clothes, and made himself much tidier than usual. Thus prepared, he went to a momentous interview.

V

The maid showed him into Lady Millicent's boudoir, where, as before, she reclined in her arm-chair, with the doll-telephone on the little table beside her.

'Well, Mr. Shovelpenny,' she said, 'your letter caused me to wonder what it can be that you wish to discuss with me. You, so I have always understood, are a brilliant man of science; I am a poor scatter-brained lady, with nothing to recommend me except a rich husband. But since I got your letter, I have taken pains to acquaint myself with your circumstances and career, and I cannot imagine that it is money you wish to see me about.'

So saying, she smiled charmingly. Shovelpenny had never before met a woman who was both rich and lovely, and he found himself somewhat disconcerted by the unexpected emotions which she roused in him. 'Come, come,' he said to himself, 'you are not here to feel emotions. You are here to conduct a grave investigation.' He pulled himself together with an effort, and replied:

'Lady Millicent, in common with the rest of mankind you must be aware of the strange commotion which has taken place throughout the human race, owing to the fear of a Martian invasion. If my information is correct, you were the first to see one of these Martians. I find it difficult to say what I have to say, but it is my duty. Careful investigation has made me doubt whether you or anybody else has seen any of these horrible creatures, and whether anything whatever is to be seen by means of the infra-redioscope. If my investigations have not misled me, I am painfully forced to the conclusion that you have been a prime mover in a gigantic fraud. I shall not be surprised if, after hearing me utter these words, you have me removed by force from your presence, and give orders to your domestics that I am not to be admitted again to your house. Such a reaction would be natural if you were innocent, and even more natural if you were guilty. But if there is any possibility that I have not thought of, if there is any way by which I can avoid condemning one so lovely as you, and one so apparently gentle as your smile proclaims you to be, if I might, throwing science to the winds, trust my instincts in your favour, then I beseech you, I implore you, for the sake of my peace of mind, let me know the whole truth!'

His obvious sincerity and his unwillingness to flatter in spite of his instinct in her favour, affected Lady Millicent as none of her usual acquaintances had ever affected her. For the first time since she had left her father to marry Sir Theophilus, she came in contact with simple sincerity. The attempt to live artificially which she had been making ever since she entered the mansion of Sir Theophilus became intolerable to her. The world of lies and schemes and intrigues and heartless power she found that she could no longer endure.

'O Mr. Shovelpenny,' she said, 'how can I answer you? I have a duty to my husband, I have a duty to mankind, and I have a duty to truth. To one at least of these I must be false. How can I decide to which of them my paramount duty is owing?'

'Lady Millicent,' he replied, 'you kindle my hope and my curiosity in equal measure. You live, as I perceive from your surroundings, an artificial life, and yet, if I am not mistaken, there is within you something that is not artificial, something sincere and simple by which you might yet be saved from the pollution that surrounds you. Speak, I implore you. Let the cleansing fire of truth purge your soul of dross!'

For a moment she was silent. Then in a firm voice she answered:

'Yes, I will speak. I have kept silence too long. I have given myself to unimaginable evil, little knowing what I was doing until, as I thought, it was too late. But you give me new hope; perhaps it is not too late; perhaps something can yet be saved—and whether anything be saved or not, I can recover that integrity which I sold to save my father from misery. Little did I know, when Sir Theophilus, in honeyed tones, and with even more than his usual conjugal blandishments, invited me to use my pictorial talents in the creation of a monster, little did I know, I repeat, in that fateful moment, for what frightful purpose the picture was required. I did as I was bid. I made the monster. I allowed myself to be quoted as having seen it, but I did not then know the fell purpose for which my husband—oh, that I must still call him such—desired me to do this deed. Step by step, as his strange campaign has unfolded itself, my conscience has troubled me more and more. Every night on my knees I have besought God to forgive me, but I know He will not do so while I am yet lapped in the luxury with which Sir Theophilus delights to surround me. Until I am willing to abandon all this, my soul cannot be purged. Your coming has been the last straw. Your coming and your simple invocation of truth has shown me at last what I must do. I will tell you all. You shall know how base is the woman to whom you are speaking. No tiniest portion of my vast turpitude will I conceal from you. And when I have stripped myself bare, perhaps I can once more feel cleansed of the foul impurity that has invaded me.'

Having so said, she told him all. As she spoke, instead of the revulsion of horror which she had expected to witness, she saw in his eyes a growing admiration, and he felt in his heart a love to which he had hitherto been a stranger. When she had told all, he took her in his arms, and she yielded to his embrace.

'Ah, Millicent,' he said, 'how tangled and how dreadful is human life. All that Hogg-Paucus told me is true, and yet, at the very fount of this evil wickedness I find you, you, who are still capable of feeling the pure flame of truth, you in whom, now that to your own ruin you have confessed all, I find a comrade, a spiritual comrade such as I did not believe the world to contain. But what to do in this strange tangle, I cannot yet decide. For twenty-four hours I must meditate. When that time has elapsed, I will come back and tell you my decision.'

When Shovelpenny returned to his apartment, he returned in a state of intellectual and emotional bewilderment, knowing neither what he felt nor what he thought. Hogg-Paucus lay on his bed, snoring in a drunken stupor. He had no wish for this man's cynicism, which he could not bring into harmony with his feelings about Millicent, whose beauty made it impossible for him to condemn her. He placed a large bottle of whisky and a glass beside Hogg-Paucus's bed, knowing that if, during the coming twenty-four hours, that worthy man should have a moment of wakefulness, the sight of the liquor would quickly overcome him, and he would return to oblivion. Having thus secured twenty-four hours without interruption, he sat down in his chair before his gas fire, and set to work to bring some kind of order into his mind.

Public and private duty alike were difficult to determine. The men who had made the plot were wicked men; their motives were vile, and they cared nothing whether mankind was the better or the worse for their activities. Private gain and private power were their sole aims. Lies, deception, and terror were their means. Could he, by his silence, make himself a party to such an infamy? And if he did not, if he persuaded Millicent to confess, as he well knew that he could, what would become of her? What would her husband do to her? What would her dupes throughout the world do to her? In imagination he saw her loveliness trampled in the dust and savage mobs tearing her to pieces. The vision was scarcely bearable, but yet, he thought, if that spark of nobility which was awakened in her while they spoke was not to be quenched anew, she must not go on living in the soft bed of profitable lies.

And so his thoughts turned to the other alternative. Should he allow Sir Theophilus and his accomplices to triumph? There were powerful arguments in favour of this course. Before the hatching of the plot, East and West had been on the verge of war, and it was thought by many that the human race would exterminate itself in futile fury. Now, from fear of a wholly imaginary danger, the real danger existed no longer. The Kremlin and the White House, united in hatred of the imaginary Martians, had become the best of friends. The armies of the world might still be mustered, but they were mustered against a foe that did not exist, and their ineffectual armaments could not do the damage for which they were intended. 'Perhaps,' so ran his meditations, 'perhaps it is only through lies that men can be induced to live sensibly. Perhaps human passions are such that to the end of time truth will be dangerous. Perhaps I have erred in giving my allegiance to truth. Perhaps Sir Theophilus is wiser than I. Perhaps it is folly in me to lead my beloved Millicent towards her ruin.'

And then his thoughts took another turn. 'Sooner or later,' so he said to himself, 'the deception will be discovered. If it is not discovered by those who, like myself, are actuated by love of truth, it will be discovered by those who have rival interests every bit as sinister as those of Sir Theophilus. What use will these men make of their discovery? They will use it only to exacerbate the revulsion against the Tellurian harmony that the lies of Sir Theophilus have engendered. Is it not better, since, sooner or later, the whole plot must be unmasked, is it not better that it should be unmasked in the name of a noble ideal, the ideal of truth, rather than in the ignoble pursuit of competition and envy? But who am I to judge such matters? I am not God. I cannot read the future. It is all dark. Wherever I look, horror stares me in the face. I know not whether to support wicked men to good ends, or good men to the destruction of the world. For that is the dreadful dilemma with which I am confronted. It is too difficult for me.'

For twenty-four hours he sat immovable in his chair, neither eating nor drinking, swayed by the to-and-fro of conflicting arguments. At the end of that time his appointment with Lady Millicent called him. He rose wearily and stiffly, sighed deeply, and with heavy steps went on foot towards her mansion.

He found Lady Millicent as shattered as he was himself. She also had been torn by perplexity. But the world played less part in her thoughts than her husband and her now dearly loved Thomas. She had not the habit of political thinking. Her world was composed of persons, persons whose activities, she knew, had various effects outside the periphery of her consciousness; but these effects she could not hope to understand. What she could understand was the human passions of the men and women who made up her private world. Throughout the twenty-four hours she had meditated on the shining qualities of Thomas's disinterestedness, with a futile and desperate wish that it had been her good fortune to come across some person possessing this character before the coils of Sir Theophilus's machinations had inextricably entwined her. She had found one thing to do which had made the suspense of those hours just bearable. She had painted from memory a miniature of Thomas, and this miniature she had placed in a locket that in more frivolous times had contained the likeness of her husband. The locket she hung on a chain round her neck, and when the suspense became unendurable she sought relief in gazing upon the likeness of him whom she yearned to call her lover.

At last he was with her, but there was no buoyancy in his step, no brightness in his eye, no resonance in his voice. Dejected and slow, he took her hand in his. With his other hand he extracted from his pocket a pill which he quickly swallowed.

'Millicent,' he said, 'this pill which I have swallowed will in a few minutes cause me to breathe no more. The choice before me is too difficult. When I was a younger man I had hopes, high hopes. I thought that I should be able to dedicate my life to the twin gods of truth and humanity. Alas! it was not to be. Shall I serve truth and cause humanity to perish, or shall I serve humanity and let truth lie trampled in the dust? O dreadful alternative! How with such a choice before me can I bear to live? How can I draw my breath beneath the sun which must either look upon carnage or be darkened by a cloud of lies? Nay, it is impossible. You, Millicent, you, you are dear to me, you believe in me, you know how true my love is . . . and yet . . . and yet. . . . What can you do for a tortured soul in such a dilemma as mine? Alas, alas, not your gentle arms, not your lovely eyes, not anything that you can offer can console me for this sorrow. No. I must die. But as I die I leave to my successors this dreadful choice—the choice between truth and life. Which to choose I know not. Goodbye, goodbye dear Millicent. I go where riddles no longer torture the guilty soul. Goodbye. . . . '

For a moment he embraced her in a last delirium of passion. She felt his heart cease to beat, and fell prostrate in momentary immobility. When she came to, she snatched the locket from her slim neck. Opening it with delicate fingers she extracted the miniature from its nest. Embracing it passionately upon the lips she exclaimed:

'O thou great spirit, thou noble mind, though thou be dead, though these lips that I vainly kiss can speak no more, yet something of thee still lives. It lives in my breast. Through me, through poor little me, the message that thou wouldst give to man shall yet be given.'

Having spoken these words she lifted the receiver of the telephone and called the *Daily Thunder*.

VI

After a few days, during which Lady Millicent was protected by the *Daily Thunder* from the fury of her husband and his minions, her story won universal belief. Everybody suddenly plucked up courage, and confessed to having seen nothing whatever through the infra-redioscope. The Martian terror subsided as quickly as it had arisen. As it subsided, the East-West dissension revived, and soon developed into open war.

The embattled nations met on the great central plain. Aeroplanes darkened the sky. Atomic explosions to right and to left scattered destruction. Vast guns of new make let loose strange missiles that sought their targets unguided by human agency. Suddenly the din stilled. The planes sank to earth. The artillery ceased to fire. On the furthest outskirts of the battle, the journalists, who had been watching with that eagerness which belongs to their strange profession, noticed the sudden silence. They could not imagine to what this silence was due. But, taking their courage in their

hands, they advanced towards what had been the battle. They found the troops dead where they had fought—dead, not by wounds inflicted by the enemy, but by some strange, new, and unknown death. They rushed to the telephones. They telephoned to their several capitals. In the capitals most widely removed from the field of battle, the stop-press got so far as to say, 'the battle has been stopped by. . . .' They got no further. When they reached this point, the compositors fell dead. The machines fell silent. Universal death spread throughout the world. The Martians *had* come.

EPILOGUE

By the Professor of Indoctrination
in the Central Martian University

I have been commissioned by that great hero whom we all revere —I allude, of course, to Martin the Conqueror—to compose the above history of the last days of the human race. That great Martian, having observed here and there among his subjects a somewhat weak-kneed sentimentality as regards those mendacious bipeds whom his hosts so gallantly and so deservedly exterminated, decided in his wisdom that all the resources of erudition should be employed to portray with exact faithfulness the circumstances preceding his victorious campaign. For he is of opinion—and I am sure that every reader of the foregoing pages will agree with him—that it could not be a good thing to allow such creatures to continue to pollute our fair cosmos.

Could anyone imagine a more foul slander than to accuse us of heptapody? And how could the Tellurians be pardoned for describing that sweet smile with which we greet changing events as a fixed grin? And what are we to think of governments which tolerate such creatures as Sir Theophilus? That love of power which led him to his enterprise is, with us, justly confined within the breast of King Martin. And what could anyone say in defence of that freedom of discussion which was shown in the debate of the United Nations? How much nobler is life on this our planet, where what is to be thought is determined by the word of the heroic Martin, and lesser men have only to obey!

The record which is here given is an authentic one. It has been pieced together with enormous labour from such fragments of newspapers and gramophone records as have survived the last Tellurian battle and the assault of our brave boys. Some may be surprised at the intimacy of some of the details that are here revealed, but it appeared that Sir Theophilus, without the knowledge of his wife, had installed a dictaphone in her boudoir, and it is from this that the last words of Mr. Shovelpenny have been derived.

Every true Martian heart must breathe more freely now in the knowledge that these creatures are no more. And in that exultant thought we shall go on to wish deserved victory to our beloved King Martin in his projected expedition against the equally degraded inhabitants of Venus.

LONG LIVE KING MARTIN!

# THE GUARDIANS OF PARNASSUS

I

In our age of wars and rumours of wars there are many who look back with nostalgia to that period of apparently unshakable stability in which their grandfathers lived what now appears like a carefree life. But unshakable stability is not to be obtained without paying a price, and I am not sure that the price was always worth paying. My father, who was already an old man when I was born, used to relate stories of those days which some of us imagine to have been golden. One in particular among his stories has helped to reconcile me to my own time.

When I (he said) was an undergraduate at Oxbridge, now very many years ago, it was my practice to take long walks in the country lanes which formerly surrounded that once beautiful city. In the course of these walks, I was frequently passed by an elderly clergyman and his daughter on horse back. Something—I knew not what—made me take note of them. The old man had an emaciated face on which I seemed to see a settled misery and a strange kind of fear—not fear of this or that, but quintessential fear, fear *per se*. Even as they rode by, it was obvious that the father and daughter were devoted to each other. She seemed to be a girl of about nineteen, but her expression was not what one expects at that age. Her appearance was far from prepossessing, but what was much more noticeable was a look of fierce determination and all but despairing defiance. I could not but wonder whether she ever smiled, whether she was ever gay, whether she ever, even for one moment, forgot whatever it was that set such a mark of inflexible purpose upon her features. After I had met the pair repeatedly, I at last inquired who the elderly clergyman was. 'Oh, that,' said my interlocutor with a laugh, 'That's the Master of Dogs' (the Master of Dogs was not a Minoan deity, but the Head of the ancient College of St. Cynicus, which undergraduates irreverently called 'Dogs'). I asked the meaning of the peculiar laugh with which this remark was accompanied. 'Do you mean to say,' said my friend, 'that you don't know the story of that old reprobate?' 'No,' I said, 'he has not the air of a criminal. What is he supposed to have done?' 'Oh, well,' said my informant, 'it's an old story now, but I'll tell it to you if you wish to hear it.' 'Yes,' I said, 'the man interests me, and so does his daughter, and I should like to know more about him.' The story I heard, which, as I afterwards learnt, was known to all the inhabitants of Oxbridge, except the younger undergraduates, was as follows:

The Master, whose name was Mr. Brown, was young in those long ago days when Fellows had to be in Orders and were not allowed to marry. He could with luck become Master, but if he was unable to achieve this his only hope of matrimony was to resign his fellowship and accept a College living, which, if a man had a family, usually involved considerable penury. The Master who preceded Mr. Brown lived to a great age, and there was considerable speculation as to who would be his successor. Mr. Brown and a certain Mr. Jones were the two whose chances appeared best. Both were engaged to be married; each hoped that his marriage would be rendered possible by the old man's death and his own subsequent election. At last the old man died. Mr. Brown and Mr. Jones entered into a chivalrous undertaking that in the ballot for the next Master each would vote for the other. Mr. Brown was elected by a majority of one. But when those who had voted for Mr. Jones inquired into the matter they became persuaded that in spite of the compact Mr. Brown had voted for himself, and that it was by this act that he had made himself Master of the College. There was no legal redress, but the Fellows of the College, including those who had previously supported Mr. Brown, decided that he should be sent to Coventry. They made known the findings of their inquiry, with the result that no one in the University would speak to him. His wife equally, though there was no evidence of her complicity, was ostracized. They had one daughter, who grew up in gloom and silence and solitude. Her mother gradually faded away and at last died of some ailment which should have been trivial. The election had happened twenty years before the time at which I heard this story, and throughout these twenty years unbending rectitude had prolonged the implacable punishment.

I was young in those days, and had not that stern devotion to moral principles which enables men to inflict torture without compunction. The story shocked me, not because of the old man's sin, but because of the concerted cruelty of the whole Oxbridge community. I did not doubt the old man's guilt. No one had doubted it for twenty years, and I could not set myself up against such a consensus, but I thought that some pity might have been shown to the daughter if not to the father. I learnt on inquiry that some ineffectual attempts had been made to befriend the girl, but that she had utterly refused to know anyone who would not know her father. I brooded on this situation until it was in danger of undermining my ethical convictions. I came almost to doubt whether punishment of sin is the main duty of the virtuous man. However, a fortuitous circumstance cut short these ethical reflections and plunged me unexpectedly from the general into the particular.

## II

On one of my lonely walks I met a horse galloping madly, and a few steps further on I saw a female figure lying by the roadside. On approaching, I found that it was the daughter of the ostracized Master. I learnt afterwards that he had been kept at home by a slight indisposition, and she had insisted on taking her usual ride, though unaccompanied. By bad luck she had met Lord George Sanger's travelling circus with elephants pulling huge vans. The elephants were too much for the nerves of the horse, which had thrown the girl and bolted. I found her conscious, but in great pain and unable to move, as she had broken a leg. At first I was at a loss as to what to do, but presently a dog-cart passed and I induced the driver, who was going to Oxbridge, to get a hospital to send an ambulance. It was about an hour and a half till the ambulance came, and during that time I did what I could to make her comfortable and show sympathy. I also let her know that I was aware of who she was.

In spite of her father's excommunication, I called next day to inquire, and learnt from the maid that when her leg was mended she would be none the worse. After this I kept myself informed of her progress, and when she was sufficiently recovered to lie on a sofa I asked if I might see her. At first she sent a message of refusal through the maid, but when, by a note, I made it clear that I was prepared to know her father, she relented. My relations with him remained formal, and he never spoke to me of his troubles. But his daughter, who had at first been as shy as a wild bird, gradually got used to me and came to rely upon my sympathy. In time I came to know all that she and her father knew of the story.

Her father in youth—so she told me—had been gay and debonair, possibly even a little wild, but so full of fun and jollity that such escapades as were suspected were readily overlooked. He was deeply in love, and overjoyed when the election made it possible for him to marry his adored Mildred. The election occurred at the very end of the Summer Term, and the marriage took place a few weeks later. Nothing compelled his return to Oxbridge until the beginning of the Autumn Term, and the couple spent the summer months in unclouded bliss. Mildred had never seen Oxbridge, which he described in glowing terms, extolling not only the architecture but the (to him) delightful society. A long vista of happiness and pleasant activity lay before them in imagination. And by this time it had become clear that in due course a child was to be expected to complete the fulfilment of their hopes.

Confidently, on his first evening in Oxbridge, the Master went to Hall to occupy his proper place at the head of the High Table. To his amazement, nobody greeted him, nobody inquired about his vacation, not a single Fellow said anything welcoming about the bride. He made some remark to Mr. A on his right, but Mr. A was so deeply engaged in conversation with *his* right-hand neighbour that he seemed not to have heard the Master. The Master had a similar experience with Mr. B on his left. After this, he was reduced to silence throughout the long dinner, while the Fellows talked and laughed with each other as if he did not exist. In spite of growing discomfort and dismay, he felt that the demands of ritual compelled him to preside over the port in the Common Room. But when he passed the port, his neighbour took it as if it had fallen from nowhere, and when it had made the round it was his neighbour, not he, who spoke across him to ask if it should make a second round. He began to doubt his own existence, and as soon as he could he went home to Mildred to be assured by her touch that he was flesh and blood and not an invisible ghost.

But no sooner had he begun to relate his strange experiences than the maid appeared with an envelope which, she said, had been dropped through the letter-box by some unknown person. Tearing open the envelope, he found inside it a long anonymous letter, obviously in a disguised hand. 'You have been judged,' it began, 'you have been judged and condemned. The law cannot touch you, but a great oath has been sworn that you shall nevertheless suffer for your sin, and that your suffering shall be as dire as any that the law inflicts upon those who outrage it.' The letter went on to relate all the damning evidence. It told of the initial reluctance of the Fellows, especially of the unsuccessful Mr. Jones, to believe that one of their number could be guilty of so dastardly an action. It told also of the minute scrutiny which, in the end, had forced conviction upon them. And it ended with a passage of almost Biblical denunciation:

'Do not imagine that by any tergiversation you will be able to shake the evidence. Do not flatter yourself that by maudlin appeals for pity you will win pardon. So long as you remain Head of this College, no Fellow will speak one word to you beyond the barest necessities of College business. Your wife, you may pretend, should not share your punishment. But she usurps the place of the lady who, but for your treachery, would now be the happy bride of Mr. Jones. So long as she continues to profit by your sin, she also must suffer retribution. With this reflection we leave you to the torments of a guilty conscience. We are

your unwilling colleagues,

The Tribunal of the Just.'

When the Master had finished this letter, he was so stunned that he took no steps to prevent his wife from reading it. At last he pulled himself together, and turned a heavy gaze upon her. 'Mildred,' he said, 'do you believe this?' Rousing herself with an effort, she answered vehemently: 'Believe it? My dearest Peter, how could you imagine such a thing? I would not believe it though all the fiends of Hell, in the likeness of Fellows of this diabolical College, should swear that they knew it with the most absolute certainty.' 'Thank you for those brave words,' he said; 'so long as they express your thoughts, my life, however painful, will not be without a refuge where human warmth is to be found. And so long as you believe in me, I shall have courage to fight this foul slander. I will not resign, for that might seem like a confession of guilt. I will devote myself to discovering the truth, and some day, somehow, it will be discovered. But, O my Love, it is hardly to be borne that you, to whom I hoped to bring all happiness, must share the life of an outcast. I would beg you to leave me, but *that* I know you will not do. The future is dark, but perhaps courage and persistence, sustained by your love, may yet lead to a happy issue.'

The Master thought, at first, that it must be possible to find some way of clearing up the mystery. He wrote to all the Fellows, solemnly asserting his innocence and demanding an inquiry. Most of them took no notice. Mr. Jones, who had been his rival, and seemed a shade less hostile than the others, replied that an inquiry had already been held: all had disclosed how they had voted, and without the Master's vote the numbers on both sides were even. It was impossible to escape the dreadful inference, and there could not be anything further to be discovered. The Master consulted lawyers and detectives, but in vain; all believed him guilty, and could suggest nothing that would diminish suspicion. Mrs. Brown, equally with her husband, was avoided by everybody, even by those few friends of her unmarried days who happened to be living in Oxbridge. The birth of a daughter, which in other circumstances would have been a joy, only added a new tragic torment: how could parents in their situation make life tolerable for the child? In a mood of despair they christened her Catherine, because they feared that she would be broken on the wheel like St. Catherine of Alexandria. They felt that it would be wanton cruelty to bring another child into this gloom. At that time and with their beliefs, this meant an end of physical relations between husband and wife. Love survived, but a love completely drained of joy.

No alleviation came with the passing years. Mrs. Brown gradually withered and at last died. Catherine, since she never heard laughter, acquired, by the time she was five years old, the sedate and silent immobility of a woman of eighty. It was impossible to send her to school, because the other children would have persecuted her. She was educated by a series of foreign governesses, who arrived from abroad in ignorance of the peculiar circumstances, and invariably gave notice as soon as they discovered them. The facts could not be kept from the girl; she would have learnt them from servants if her parents had been silent. Her father, especially after his wife's death, lavished tenderness upon her, in a vain endeavour to compensate her in some measure for her social isolation. She in return gave him all that wealth of affection which, in a more normal childhood, is distributed among many. As she reached years of discretion, she became consumed by a burning passion to vindicate her father and make visible to all the world the inhuman cruelty of the sentence passed upon him by judges of whose injustice she felt no doubt. But father and daughter alike were helpless. Their affection for each other, in the narrow compass left by a hostile world, could not be warm and comforting; each was stabbed by awareness of the other's suffering, and each felt, though neither said, that the agony would be less unendurable without the spectacle of the other's misery.

This history became known to me bit by bit in the course of several visits to Catherine during her convalescence. I found myself quite unable to disbelieve her version, and at the same time quite unable to account for the evidence against her father. If her father was innocent, as she claimed, there was a mystery, pointing to something undiscovered. I would have investigated events at the time of the election if I could have thought of any way of bringing some hidden fact to light, but after so many years that seemed impossible. However, in the middle of my perplexities, the truth suddenly came to light, complete, astounding, and terrible.

## III

Soon after Catherine's recovery became complete, her father died. This was no surprise, as the misery of his life had gradually worn him down. What was a surprise was the death a few days later of his bitterest enemy in the College, Dr. Greatorex, the Professor of Pastoral Theology. The surprise became amazement when it was found that the death was a suicide and that the Professor had taken poison. He had been, all his life, an implacable enemy of sin and a firm pillar of rectitude. He was deeply admired by elderly maiden ladies whose virtue had become somewhat sour, and he was thought well of by all those eminent academic personages who had been untouched by the softening of moral codes which characterizes our enfeebled age. His professorship, it was felt, served to keep alive in the University such standards as would cause parents to feel that their sons were in safe hands. In the days before the election to the Mastership he had been the most vehement opponent of Dr. Brown and the most whole-hearted advocate of Mr. Jones. When Dr. Brown was declared elected, it was Dr. Greatorex who first instigated an inquiry, and it was through his efforts that the Master's guilt came to be universally believed. When the Master died, no one supposed that Dr. Greatorex would feel much grief. Still less could they have imagined that this man of blameless life would end his days by committing a mortal sin. He had, it is true, shocked even some of his admirers by a sermon which he preached in the College Chapel on the Sunday following the Master's death. He took for his text, 'Where their worm dieth not, and the fire is not quenched.' He pointed out that some careless readers of the Gospels have represented Our Lord as very ready to forgive sinners, and have even hinted that He perhaps did not teach their eternal damnation. The learned Professor pointed out that the text on which he was preaching occurs in St. Mark's gospel, and cannot be explained away in any honest attempt to understand the teaching of the Gospels. So far, his sermon could win approval; but what pained his hearers and seemed to them, in the circumstances, a failure in good taste, was the fact that the eternal punishment of sinners was to him a matter of satisfaction and, what was worse, that he obviously had the late Master in mind. Theology, it was felt, is all very well in its place, but it cannot supersede the demands of good taste. Everybody went away from the sermon somewhat chilled. Mr. Jones, who had always been reluctant in the condemnation of his successful rival, decided to pay a visit to Professor Greatorex and to suggest to him that perhaps now the time for denunciation was passed. In the evening he knocked on the Professor's door, but received no answer. He knocked again, more loudly, and at last, seeing that the Professor's light was on, he feared that something might be amiss, and entered. The Professor was sitting at his desk, dead, with a bulky manuscript before him addressed to the Coroner. Mr. Jones himself did not think fit to read this manuscript, but handed it to the police, who caused it to be read at the inquest. In this statement Professor Greatorex said:

'My life's work is nearly complete. It remains only to tell the world what it was, and in what manner I was an instrument in the punishment of sin. Brown and I were friends in youth. He was in those days bolder and more adventurous than I. We both intended to take Orders and to adopt an academic career, but in the meanwhile we permitted ourselves some of those enjoyments which, after Ordination, might be thought unseemly. There was a certain tobacconist with whom we both dealt, and this tobacconist had a lovely daughter named Muriel, who sometimes served in the shop. She had bright eyes, mischievous and inviting. She was sprightly in badinage with undergraduates, but I felt that behind the façade there was a person of great feeling and capacity for profound affection. I fell deeply in love with her, but I knew that marriage was incompatible with an academic career, and that marriage to a tradesman's daughter would be a black mark against me in any other career for which I was fitted. I was then, as I have been throughout my life, inflexibly determined to abstain from carnal sin, and I never for a moment contemplated the possibility of an immoral relation with Muriel. But Brown had no such scruples. While I hesitated, torn between ambition and love, Brown acted. By his carefree gaiety he won the poor girl's heart and led her by his wiles into sin. I alone knew of this, and the torments that I suffered in the spectacle of Muriel's ruin are beyond the power of language to depict. I expostulated with Brown, but in vain. Muriel, aware of my knowledge of her guilty secret, cajoled me into a vow of silence. After some months, she disappeared. I did not know what had happened to her, but I darkly suspected that Brown did not share my ignorance. In this, however, I was mistaken. After a period of agonizing unhappiness, I received a letter from her, written from a miserable lodging in a slum, confessing that she was pregnant, that she loved Brown too much to embarrass him, and that she had therefore not let him know of her condition or her whereabouts. Reminding me of my vow of secrecy, she asked if I could help her until the birth of her child, which was imminent. I visited her and found her in desperate penury, not having dared to make confession to her father, whose morals were as stern as my own. Fortunately this was during the vacation, and I was able to be absent from Oxbridge without exciting comment. I gave her assistance, and when her time came I secured for her a bed in a hospital. She and the child both died. I repented vainly my former prudence. My vow, which she had induced me to renew, made it impossible to reveal Brown's infamy. What had become of her he never knew, and I am convinced that he never cared.

'Although I could not expose him, I determined to devote my life to punishing him in whatever way circumstances might make possible. In the contest for the Mastership, I found my opportunity. I was the most vehement supporter of Mr. Jones, and I could have secured his election. But Brown would have survived the disappointment, and his suffering would have been in no degree commensurate with Muriel's. I suddenly conceived a more subtle vengeance. In the ballot, I voted for Brown. Nobody had for a moment imagined that this could happen, and in the scrutiny it was accepted, with little prompting from me, that my vote had gone to Jones. As I had foreseen, Brown's election appeared to have resulted from his voting for himself. I did not abstain from such words as would inflame feeling against him. Everything worked as I had planned, and his years of anguish began, an anguish which, I am happy to think, was much longer and much more bitter than any that Muriel had had to endure. I watched the roses fade from his wife's cheeks, I saw her sink into listless despair, and I thought with joy, "Muriel, you are avenged." I had a daguerreotype of Brown, made when he was young and jolly. Every evening before saying my prayers I took out this daguerreotype and gloated over the change made by Brown's sunken cheeks and haunted eyes. In later years, I watched with glee the poison of isolation filling his love for his daughter with unhealthy morbidness. His misery made my life; and, in comparison, nothing else was important to me. In comparison with the magnitude of my hate, the little emotions of my colleagues have seemed trivial. I have not known the joys of love, but I have known the joys of hate; and who shall say which are the greater? But now my enemy is dead, and I have nothing left to live for on earth. Faith, however, supplies me with a hope. I shall perish by my own hand, and shall therefore spend eternity in Hell. There I shall hope to find Brown, and, if there is justice in Hell, ways will be vouchsafed to me of increasing the horror of his everlasting torments. In this hope I die.'

# BENEFIT OF CLERGY

### I

Penelope Colquhoun climbed slowly up the stairs and sank wearily into an uncomfortable wicker chair in her tiny sitting-room. 'Oh, I am bored, I am bored, I am bored,' she said out loud with a deep sigh.

It must be confessed that she had reason for this feeling. Her father was the vicar of a remote parish in rural Suffolk, the name of which was Quycombe Magna. The village consisted of the church, the vicarage, a post office, a public house, ten cottages, and—its only redeeming feature—a fine old Manor House. Its only connection with the outer world at that time, some fifty years since, was a bus which ran three times a week to Quycombe Parva, a much larger village, with a railway station from which (it was said) persons of sufficient longevity might hope to reach Liverpool Street.

Penelope's father, who had been for five years a widower, was of a type now nearly extinct, low-church, bigoted, and opposed to every kind of enjoyment. His wife had been all that, in his opinion, a wife should be: submissive, patient, and indefatigable in parish work. He took it for granted that Penelope would follow unquestioningly in the footsteps of her sainted mother. Having no alternative, she did her best. She decorated the church for Christmas and the Harvest Festival; she presided over the Mothers' Meeting; she visited old women and inquired about their ailments; she scolded the verger if he neglected his duties. No chink of pleasure was allowed to lighten her routine. The vicar frowned upon adornment of the female person. She wore always woollen stockings and a severe coat and skirt, presumably new once, but now shabby. Her hair was pulled tightly back from the forehead. No kind of ornament had ever been imagined, since her father would have thought it the inevitable gateway to hell. Except for a charwoman for two hours in the mornings, she had no domestic help, and had to do the cooking and housework in addition to the parish duties normally performed by vicars' wives.

She had, on occasion, made ineffectual efforts to achieve a little liberty; but in vain. Her father was always able to cite a text proving conclusively that her demands were wicked. He was particularly fond of Ecclesiasticus, which, as he was wont to point out, could be cited for edification though not for doctrine. Once, shortly after her mother's death, an itinerant fair came to Quycombe Magna and she asked if she might be allowed to see it. He replied, 'Whoso taketh pleasure in wickedness shall be condemned: but he that resisteth pleasure crowneth his life.' Once it was discovered that she had exchanged a few words with a passing cyclist who had asked the way to Ipswich. Her father was deeply shocked and said: 'She that is bold dishonoureth both her father and her husband, but they both shall despise her.' When she protested that the conversation had been harmless, he said that unless she reformed he would not allow her to go about the village alone, and reinforced the threat by the text: 'If thy daughter be shameless, keep her in straitly, lest she abuse herself through over much liberty.' She was fond of music and would have liked to have a piano, but her father considered this unnecessary, saying, 'Wine and music will rejoice the heart, but the love of wisdom is above them both.' He was never tired of explaining how much anxiety he had on her account. He would say, 'The father waketh for the daughter, when no man knoweth, and the care for her taketh away sleep. . . . For from garments cometh a moth, and from women wickedness.'

The five years that followed her mother's death had driven Penelope to the very verge of what she could endure. At last, when she reached the age of twenty, a tiny crack opened in her prison walls. The Manor House, which had stood empty for some years, was again inhabited by the lady of the Manor, Mrs. Menteith. She was American and well-to-do. Her husband, who could not endure vegetating in East Anglia, had gone out to Ceylon. She had returned from Ceylon to find schools for her sons and to see about letting the Manor House. The vicar could not wholly approve of her, as she was gay and well dressed, and what he would consider worldly. But, as the Manor House contributed by far the largest subscription to church expenses, he found a text in Ecclesiasticus about the unwisdom of offending the rich, and did not forbid his daughter to know the lively lady.

No sooner had Penelope finished sighing over her boredom than she heard a knock on the old-fashioned knocker on the front door of the vicarage, and on going down she found Mrs. Menteith on the doorstep. A few sympathetic words brought an outburst from Penelope which touched Mrs. Menteith's heart. Looking at the girl with the eye of a connoisseur, she perceived possibilities that neither the girl herself nor anybody in the parish had suspected. 'My dear,' she said, 'do you realize that if you were free to take a little trouble, you could be a raving beauty?' 'Oh, Mrs. Menteith,' said the girl, 'surely you are joking!' 'No,' said the lady, 'I am not. And, if we can outwit your father, I will prove it.' After some further conversation, they hatched a plot. At this moment Mr. Colquhoun came in and Mrs. Menteith said, 'Dear Mr. Colquhoun, I wonder if you could spare your daughter to me for just one day. I have a lot of tiresome business to do in Ipswich and I shall find the time intolerably tedious if I have to be alone. You will be doing me a great kindness, if you allow your daughter to accompany me in my car.' Somewhat reluctantly and after some further blandishment, the vicar consented. The great day came, and Penelope could hardly contain herself for excitement. 'Your father,' said Mrs. Menteith, 'is an old horror, and I am thinking out a scheme by which in time you may be liberated from his tyranny. When we get to Ipswich I will dress you from head to foot in the most becoming clothes that I can find there. I will have your hair done as it should be done. I think the result will surprise you.' It certainly did. When Penelope saw herself dressed to satisfy Mrs. Menteith, she looked in the long mirror and thought, 'Is this really me?' She became completely lost in a daze of nascent vanity. A whole flood of new emotions crowded in upon her. New hopes and undreamt of possibilities made her determine to be done with the life of a drudge. But the manner of escape still remained an unsolved problem.

While she was still brooding, Mrs. Menteith took her to the beauty parlour to have her hair done. She had to wait some time, and her eye fell upon a copy of *The Matrimonial News*. 'Mrs. Menteith,' she said, 'you are doing so much for me that I hesitate to ask one further favour—What will be the use of looking beautiful if nobody ever sees me? And at Quycombe Magna, no young men are to be seen from one year's end to another. Will you allow me to put an advertisement in *The Matrimonial News* giving the Manor House as my address, and interviewing there any applicant who seems worth seeing?' Mrs. Menteith, who by this time was thoroughly enjoying the fun, agreed. And Penelope, with her help, drew up the following advertisement:

> Young woman, of great beauty and impeccable virtue, but isolated in remote country district, wishes to meet young man with a view to matrimony. Applicants to enclose photograph and, if viewed favourably, young woman's photograph will be sent in return. Reply: Miss P., Manor House, Quycombe Magna. P.S.—No clergy need apply.

Having dispatched this advertisement, she underwent the ministrations of the beauty parlour and was then photographed in all her splendour. For the moment, this ended the dream of glory. She had to take off all her fine clothes and brush her hair back into its previous straight severity. But the fine clothes went back with Mrs. Menteith to the Manor House with the promise that she should wear them in interviewing applicants.

When she got home, she put on a weary expression, and told her father how bored she'd been while waiting in the anterooms of solicitors and house agents. 'Penelope,' said her father, 'you were doing a kindness to Mrs. Menteith, and the virtuous are never bored when doing a kindness.' She accepted this observation with becoming meekness, and prepared herself to wait with what patience she could command for such replies as her advertisement might bring forth.

II

The replies to Penelope's advertisement were many and various. Some were earnest, some facetious; some explained that the writer was rich, or else that he was so clever that he soon would be rich; some, it was possible to suspect, hoped that matrimony might be avoided; some emphasized their good nature, others their powers of domination. Penelope, whenever she could, went to the Manor House to collect the answers. But there was only one among them all that she felt to be promising:

Dear Miss P.,
 Your advertisement intrigues me. Few women would have the nerve to claim great beauty, and only a small proportion of these would at the same time claim impeccable virtue. I am trying to reconcile this with your aversion from the clerical profession, which permits the glimmer of a hope that your virtue is not more impeccable than becomes a young woman. I am consumed with curiosity, and, if you give me a chance to gratify it, you will increase my felicity.
       Yours expectantly,
         PHILIP ARLINGTON

P.S.—I enclose my photograph.

This letter intrigued her. The writer's complete silence as to his own merits made her suppose them so great that he could take them for granted. In the photograph, he looked lively and intelligent, with a considerable sense of fun and a not unpleasing dash of roguery. To him alone she replied, enclosing a photograph of herself in all her finery and suggesting a day on which she could meet him for lunch at the Manor House. He accepted. The day came.

The Manor House and Mrs. Menteith's presence at lunch gave a favourable impression of Penelope's respectability and social status. After lunch they were left alone to make each other's acquaintance. He began by observing that in the matter of beauty her advertisement had claimed no more than the truth, and he expressed surprise that she had resorted to such a medium in the search for a husband, which (so he was pleased to say) should have been all too easy. This led her to explain her domestic circumstances, including the grounds of her objection to the clergy. With every moment she found his half-humorous sympathy more agreeable, and became more convinced that life as his wife would be in all respects the opposite of life as her father's daughter.

At the end of two hours' *tête-à-tête*, she was already in love with him and, so far as she could judge, he was by no means indifferent to her. She then broached the problem which had been troubling her. 'I am,' she said, 'only twenty years of age and cannot yet marry without my father's consent. He will never consent to my marrying a man who is not in Orders. Do you think that when I introduce you to him, you could convincingly pose as a clergyman?' At this question, a queer twinkle appeared in his eyes, which she found somewhat puzzling, but he replied reassuringly, 'Yes, I think I can manage that.' She was delighted to have him as a partner in the hoodwinking of her father, and felt more at one with him than ever. She spoke of him to her father as a friend of Mrs. Menteith's whom she had happened to meet at the Manor House. Her father was naturally upset at the thought of losing a domestic drudge who demanded no wages, but Mrs. Menteith backed up Penelope in glowing accounts of the young man's exemplary piety and of the

chances of future preferment which he owed to several episcopal patrons. At last the old man reluctantly consented to inspect this paragon, and to permit the engagement if the inspection proved satisfactory. Penelope was in tenter-hooks for fear her dear Philip should make some slip which would enable her father to discover the deception. But, to her bewildered joy, everything went off without a hitch. The young man spoke of the parish in which he was curate, described his vicar, mentioned that he had taken Orders because of the family living in which the present incumbent was ninety years of age, and wound up with a glowing peroration about the importance and sacredness of the work to which he hoped to dedicate his life. Penelope secretly gasped, but observed with amusement that her father's opinion of Philip grew with leaps and bounds, reaching its acme when the young man actually quoted Ecclesiasticus.

All the difficulties being thus smoothed away, the marriage took place in a few weeks. They went to Paris for their honeymoon, she explaining that she had had enough of the country and, when pleasure was the object, preferred populous gaiety to the beauties of nature. The honeymoon was to her one long dream of delight. Her husband was invariably charming and never objected to the many forms of frivolity which her abstemious years had compelled her hitherto to repress. There was only one cloud on the horizon. He was very reticent about himself, but explained that for financial reasons he was compelled to live in the village of Poppleton in Somerset. And from his talk about the neighbouring grand house, inhabited by Sir Rostrevor and Lady Kenyon, she supposed that he must be their agent. But, although she wondered at times that he was not more explicit, every moment of the honeymoon was so filled with pleasure that she had little time to brood on the matter. He explained that he must reach Poppleton on a certain Saturday. They arrived very late at The Rye House where he lived. It was too dark and she was too weary to wish for anything but sleep at the moment. He led her upstairs, and she fell asleep as soon as her head touched the pillow.

III

She awoke next morning to the sound of church bells and to the sight of her husband putting on clerical attire. This sight made her instantly wide awake. 'What *are* you putting on those clothes for!' she exclaimed. 'Well, my dear,' he replied with a smile, 'the time has come to make a little confession. When I first saw your advertisement I felt nothing but curiosity, and it was only for fun that I suggested an interview. But, as soon as I saw you, I loved you. And every moment at the Manor House deepened this feeling. I determined to win you and, since this was impossible by fair means, I used foul ones. I can no longer conceal from you that I am a curate in this parish. That I have basely deceived you is true. My only excuse is the greatness of my love, which could not have won you in any other way.'

At this she leapt from her bed, exclaiming, 'I shall never forgive you! Never! Never! Never! But I will make you repent. I will make you rue the day that you treated a poor girl in this infamous manner. I will make you, and as many as possible of your clerical accomplices, as much of a laughing stock as you have made me.' By this time he was fully dressed. She pushed him out of the door, locked it, and remained in solitary dudgeon throughout the rest of the day.

He gave no sign of his presence until supper time, when he knocked on her door with a tray saying, 'If you're going to punish me, you must keep alive; and if you're to keep alive, you must eat. So here's a tray. But you needn't speak to me. I'll put it on the floor and go away. *Bon appétit!*' At first she wanted to be proud, but she had had no breakfast and no lunch and no tea. And at last hunger overcame her, and she devoured everything on the tray. Nevertheless, she did not abandon her scheme of revenge.

Refreshed by her supper, she spent the evening composing a dignified letter to him, outlining a *modus vivendi* for the immediate future. She took great pains with this letter, and made several drafts of it. But in the end she was satisfied. In the final draft she said:

> Sir,
> You will, of course, realize that, in view of your infamous behaviour, I shall never again speak an unnecessary word to you. I shall not tell the world what you have done to me, for that would be to lay bare my own folly; but I shall make it clear to all the world that I do not love you, that you were infatuated, and that any other man would do as well. I shall delight in causing scandal because it will reflect on your judgment. And if, in doing so, I can bring clerics into disrepute, my pleasure will be enhanced. My only aim in life, henceforth, will be to inflict upon you a humiliation as profound as that which you have inflicted upon me. Your wife, henceforth in name only,
>
> PENELOPE

She put the letter on the supper tray, and put the supper tray outside her door.

Next morning another tray appeared, containing not only a delicious breakfast, but also a note. At first she thought she would tear it into little pieces and throw the little pieces out of the window. But she could not resist the hope that he would be overwhelmed with sorrow and shame, and would make such apology as the circumstances allowed. She tore open the letter and read:

Bravo, dearest Penelope! Your letter is a masterpiece in dignified reproach. I doubt if I could have improved it if you had asked my advice. But as for revenge, my dear, we shall see. It may not work out quite as you are thinking. Still your clerical admirer,

PHILIP

P.S.—Don't forget the garden party.

The garden party in question, of which Philip had spoken during the honeymoon, was to be given that day by Sir Rostrevor and Lady Kenyon at their lovely Elizabethan mansion Mendip Place. The date had been fixed partly with a view to introducing the bride to the county. For some time she hesitated as to whether she should go, her husband's postscript inclining her towards the negative. But after some deliberation she decided that the party would afford her an opportunity of inaugurating her revenge. She dressed with the utmost care. Indignation lent a sparkle to her looks, which made them even more irresistible than usual. She decided that it would further her ends to conceal her quarrel with her husband, and they arrived together with the utmost correctness. Her beauty was so dazzling that all the men who saw her forgot everything else. She, however, put on a demure and simple demeanour, and, ignoring the grand people who sought introductions to her, devoted her attentions almost exclusively to the vicar. The vicar, whose name was Mr. Reverdy, was a man of young middle age, and Penelope discovered within a few minutes that he had a passion for local archaeology. He told her with great earnestness that there was in the neighbourhood a Long Barrow probably full of the most valuable prehistoric relics, but that he alone was interested in it, and no one could be induced to dig it up. She looked at him with great eyes and said, 'Oh, Mr. Reverdy, what a shame!' He was so impressed that he congratulated his curate upon having found such a perfect soul-mate.

He managed to persuade Penelope (though, as he supposed, with some difficulty) to go next day in his carriage to view certain interesting archaeological remains at a distance of about ten miles from Poppleton. They were seen driving together through the village, he in very earnest conversation and she with an air of rapt attention. They were, of course, seen by everybody. But especially by a certain old lady named Mrs. Quigley, who made the purveying of gossip her business. Mrs. Quigley had a daughter whom she had destined for dear Mr. Arlington, and she began to see reason to doubt the wisdom of his neglect of this excellent spinster. As the vicar and Penelope drove by, Mrs. Quigley said, 'Humph!' And all those who heard her understood the meaning of this monosyllable. But worse was to follow. Next morning, at a moment when Mr. Arlington was known to be occupied with parish duties, the vicar was seen marching up to The Rye House, carrying a large tome on the archaeology of Somerset. And he was observed to stay for a considerably longer time than the mere delivery of the volume would require. Backstairs gossip revealed to Mrs. Quigley, and therefore to the whole village, that the newly married couple occupied separate rooms.

The poor vicar, meanwhile, not yet aware of Mrs. Quigley's activities, babbled to everybody about the beauty, intelligence, and virtue of his curate's wife. And with every word that he uttered, he increased the gravamen of the charges against himself as well as her. At last Mrs. Quigley could bear it no longer and felt it her duty to write to Mr. Glasshouse, the Rural Dean, suggesting that for the sake of the dear vicar it would be well if a cure could be found elsewhere for the curate. Mr. Glasshouse, who knew Mrs. Quigley, was not inclined to take the matter very seriously, and thought that a word in season to the vicar was all that would be necessary. He visited the vicar, who assured him that nothing in the world could be more innocent than the few dealings that he had had with Mrs. Arlington. He, however, praised her innocence somewhat more warmly than the Rural Dean thought quite fitting. And Mr. Glasshouse decided to view the lady for himself.

He arrived at The Rye House at tea time, and was warmly welcomed by Penelope, who was beginning to get a little tired of archaeology and the vicar. It must, however, be confessed that when Mr. Glasshouse, with great delicacy, approached the subject of the scandalous rumours retailed to him by Mrs. Quigley, Penelope, though she denied everything, did it in such a manner as to convince

Mr. Glasshouse that the vicar had been at least indiscreet. Mr. Glasshouse by this time had confessed that archaeology was too much concerned with the dead past to suit his taste, and that for his part he preferred life to dead stones. 'Oh, Mr. Glasshouse,' she replied, 'how right you are, and how wholly I agree with you. Do tell me, dear Dean, what forms of life particularly interest you.' 'Rare birds,' he replied, 'especially those that frequent the fens of Sedgemoor, where not only are kingfishers common, but even yellow water-wagtails reward the patient watcher.' Clasping her hands together, and looking up at him enthusiastically, she explained that in spite of living in the neighbourhood of the Norfolk fens, and in spite of many journeys of exploration, she had never yet been gratified in her longing to see a yellow water-wagtail.

The Rural Dean, sad as it is to relate, forgot his mission, forgot his duty to the diocese, forgot his sacred calling, and invited her to join him in watching for the yellow water-wagtail in a lonely spot that he knew to be one of its favourite haunts. 'Oh, Mr. Dean,' she replied, 'what *will* Mrs. Quigley say?' He did his best to put on the airs of the man of the world, and brushed aside that virtuous matron as a woman of no account. Before he could finish the second cup of tea, Penelope had yielded to his vehemence and agreed to join him in an expedition on the first fine day. They went. But, lonely as the spot was, Mrs. Quigley's spies were at work. Before long she knew the worst, and more. Seeing that the Church had failed her, she attempted to secure the help of Lady Kenyon, assuring her that from the reports she had received it was not only birds that the Rural Dean had observed. 'I will not say more,' she added, 'for that is too easy to imagine. Can you, dear Lady, exorcise this Siren who is turning from the path of duty even the most staid and highly respected of our religious mentors?' Lady Kenyon replied that she would think it over and see what she could do. Knowing Mrs. Quigley, she thought that it might be wise to get a more first-hand report as to the facts, so she called on Penelope and asked what all the fuss was about.

After a little coaxing, she got the whole story out of Penelope. But, instead of taking the story tragically, Lady Kenyon merely laughed. 'Oh, my dear girl,' she said, 'what you're doing is really too easy. How can you expect these stuffy old men to resist you? Why, they've never seen a really beautiful woman in their lives until they saw you. . . .' 'Except yourself,' interjected Penelope. But Lady Kenyon ignored the interjection, and went on as if Penelope had not spoken. 'No, my dear, if your revenge is to be worth anything, it must be practised on someone worthy of your mettle. The Bishop of Glastonbury, whose clergy you have been leading along the primrose path, is worthy of your steel. I should not wonder if in him you were to meet your match. I will arrange a tournament between you and him, and I myself will "rain influence and judge the prize"—with complete impartiality I assure you, for, though I greatly admire the Bishop, I cannot but enjoy your adventurous spirit.'

IV

The Bishop of Glastonbury was a man of considerable scholastic eminence, which had enabled him to rise in the clerical profession in spite of what some considered a regrettable frivolity. Although no real scandal had ever been fastened upon him, he was known to be fond of the society of charming ladies and not always wholly serious in his converse with them. Lady Kenyon, who knew him well, told him all that she had gathered about Penelope and the havoc that she was wreaking on his clergy. 'The girl,' she said, 'is not really bad, but only very angry. And it must be admitted that she has cause for anger. I was unable to exert a good influence upon her, partly, I think, because her story amused me and I could not find it in my heart to scold her. But you, my dear Bishop, will, I am convinced, succeed where I have failed. If you are willing, I will get her to meet you here, and we shall see what we shall see.'

The Bishop agreed; and Penelope was duly invited to meet him at Mendip Place. Recent experience had given her confidence, and she did not doubt that she would be able to turn the Bishop round her little finger. She duly told him her tale, but was somewhat disconcerted by the fact that he smiled at the most pathetic parts. And when she looked up at him with adoring eyes, such as no vicar or Rural Dean could resist, to her horror he merely winked. The wink made her change her tone, and she became simple and sincere. The Bishop elicited from her that, in spite of furious anger, she still loved Philip, but pride would not allow her to admit it to him. 'My dear,' said the Bishop, who was treating her affectionately but not seriously, 'I don't think your present course is likely to bring you much satisfaction. The world is full of silly men ready to fall in love with you, but you cannot love a silly man. And no man who is not silly can fail to see that your husband holds your heart. He has, of course, played an all but unforgivable trick upon you, and I do not suggest that you should behave as if nothing had happened. But I think that if you are ever to achieve any happiness, you must find something better to do than bemusing foolish parsons. What you should do is for you to decide, but it should be something more positive and satisfying than revenge.' With that he patted her hand and said, 'Think it over, my dear, and in due course let me know your decision.'

She went home somewhat deflated, and realizing for the first time that a noble wrath is in the long run an unsatisfying diet. There were difficult practical decisions to be made if she altered her way of life. She was not prepared to surrender to the point of becoming the submissive wife of a country curate, still less was she prepared to go back to her father. She must therefore find some way of earning a living. In a long letter to Mrs. Menteith, she related what had happened to her since her marriage, ending with the Bishop's friendly admonition.

> 'From you,' she ended, 'I have had so much kindness that I hesitate to ask even more. But I feel that perhaps you could help me to find my feet. Would you be willing to meet me in London to talk things over?'

They met and, in consequence, Mrs. Menteith persuaded her own dressmaker to take on Penelope as a mannequin. When she moved to London, she ceased to have any communication with her husband.

Poppleton forgot her. And no one missed her except Mrs. Quigley —and possibly her husband, though his feelings were never expressed. Her beauty made her an asset to the dressmaker, and it was gradually discovered that she had great talent as a dress designer. She rose rapidly, and within three years was earning a very comfortable salary. She was about to be taken into partnership, when she received a doleful letter from her father saying that he was very unwell and feared he was dying:

> 'You have behaved very ill,' he said, 'both to me and to your worthy husband. But I wish all ill-feeling to end before I die, and for this reason I shall be glad if you will return for however brief a space to your old home.
> 'In all Christian love,
>
> YOUR FATHER

With a heavy heart she went to Liverpool Street. As she was looking for a seat, she saw—but could it be?—her husband, not in clerical dress, looking very prosperous and about to get into a first-class carriage. For a moment they stared at each other. Then she exclaimed, 'Philip!' And at the very same moment he exclaimed, 'Penelope!' 'My dear, you are lovelier than ever,' he said. 'Philip,' she replied, 'what has become of those clothes that caused our rupture?' 'They are left to the care of moth balls,' he replied. 'I discovered that I have talent as an inventor, so I gave up the Church. I have a very good income, and am on my way to visit the Cambridge Scientific Instrument Makers about a new patent. But how about you? You don't look exactly poverty-stricken.' 'No,' she said, 'I, too, have prospered.' And she related her successful career. 'I always thought you were no fool,' he said. 'And I always thought you were a knave,' she replied, 'but now I no longer mind.' With that they fell into each other's arms on the platform. 'Jump in, Sir and Madam,' said the guard. And they lived happy ever after.

THE END

## NIGHTMARES
### of Eminent Persons

If *Satan in the Suburbs*, Bertrand Russell's first work of fiction, had been received merely as a philosopher's aberration, he would probably not have been encouraged to write any more stories. But it was one of the successful books of its year.

This new collection begins with a series of Nightmares dreamt by such eminent persons as Stalin and the Queen of Sheba. These, Bertrand Russell says, might be called Signposts to Sanity, since "the man who wishes to preserve sanity in a dangerous world should summon in his mind a parliament of fears, in which each in turn is voted absurd by all the others. The dreamers of these nightmares did not adopt this technique; it is hoped that the reader will have more wisdom!"

Bertrand Russell has added two longer stories to complete a volume which will be welcomed by all those who enjoyed his earlier book. Charles Stewart's illustrations perfectly capture the macabre atmosphere of those horrific dreams.

ISBN 0 85124 629 X £7.99, 150pp
Available from Spokesman

Books by
# Bertrand Russell
available from Spokesman

### Portraits from Memory
A series of brilliant pen portraits including, among others Bernard Shaw, H. G. Wells, Joseph Conrad, and D. H. Lawrence.

ISBN 0 85124 582 X - paper, £9.99

ISBN 0 85124 581 1 - cloth, £30.00 - 228pp

### The Practice and Theory of Bolshevism
An essential text for all of Russell's many admirers, and for everyone who wishes to understand the beginnings of Soviet power and politics, which also offers insights in to some of the problems which dog modern Russia.

ISBN 0 85124 541 2 – paper, £7.99

ISBN 0 85124 – cloth, £30.00 - 136pp

**All these titles are available from Spokesman Books, Russell House, Bulwell Lane, Nottingham. NG6 0BT, from whom a full list is available on request.**

www.spokesmanbooks.com

Books by
# Bertrand Russell
available from
Spokesman

## The Problem of China

The story of a fascinating encounter with China and its people, originally published in 1922, following the author's return 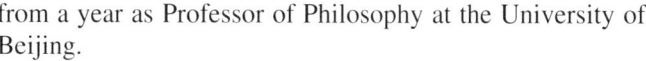 from a year as Professor of Philosophy at the University of Beijing.

ISBN 0 85124 553 6 - paper, £8.95

ISBN 0 85124 552 8 - cloth, £30.00 - 260pp

## German Social Democracy

Bertrand Russell's first book (published in 1896) comprised six lectures delivered at the London School of Economics in the early months of that year. When it was last re-printed, in 1965, Russell wrote that he had "left it as an historical document in which a former writer comments on a former world."

ISBN 0 85124 571 4 - paper, £9.99

ISBN 0 85124 570 6 - cloth, £35.00 - 192pp

All these titles are available from Spokesman Books, Russell House, Bulwell Lane, Nottingham. NG6 0BT, from whom a full list is available on request.

www.spokesmanbooks.com

# BY BERTRAND RUSSELL

| | |
|---|---|
| 1896 | *German Social Democracy* (available from Spokesman) |
| 1897 | *An Essay on the Foundations of Geometry* |
| 1900 | *The Philosophy of Leibniz* |
| 1903 | *The Principles of Mathematics* |
| 1910 | *Philosophical Essays* |
| 1910 | *Principia Mathematica Vol.I* (with A.N. Whitehead), *Vol.II* 1911, *Vol.III* 1913 |
| 1912 | *Problems with Philosophy* |
| 1914 | *Our Knowledge of the External World* |
| 1916 | *Justice in Wartime* |
| 1916 | *Principles of Social Reconstruction* |
| 1917 | *Political Ideals* |
| 1918 | *Roads to Freedom* |
| 1918 | *Mysticism and Logic* |
| 1919 | *Introduction to Mathematical Philosophy* |
| 1920 | *The Practice and Theory of Bolshevism* (available from Spokesman) |
| 1921 | *The Analysis of Mind* |
| 1922 | *The Problem of China* (available from Spokesman) |
| 1923 | *Prospects of Industrial Civilisation* (with Dora Russell) |
| 1923 | *The ABC of Atoms* |
| 1924 | *Icarus or the Future of Science* |
| 1925 | *The ABC of Relativity* |
| 1925 | *What I Believe* |
| 1926 | *On Education* |
| 1927 | *Selected Papers of Betrand Russell* |
| 1927 | *An Outline of Philosophy* |
| 1927 | *The Analysis of Matter* |
| 1928 | *Sceptical Essays* |
| 1929 | *Marriage and Morals* |
| 1930 | *The Conquest of Happiness* |
| 1931 | *The Scientific Outlook* |
| 1932 | *Education and the Social Order* |
| 1934 | *Freedom and Organisation 1814-1914* |
| 1935 | *In Praise of Idleness* |
| 1935 | *Religion and Science* |
| 1936 | *Which Way to Peace?* |
| 1937 | *The Amberley Papers* (with Patricia Russell) |
| 1938 | *Power* |
| 1940 | *An Inquiry into Meaning and Truth* |
| 1945 | *History of Western Philosophy* |
| 1948 | *Human Knowledge: Its Scope and Limits* |
| 1949 | *Authority and the Individual* |
| 1950 | *Unpopular Essays* |
| 1951 | *New Hope for a Changing World* |
| 1951 | *The Wit and Wisdom of Bertrand Russell* (ed. L. Denonn) |
| 1952 | *The Impact of Science on Society* |

| | |
|---|---|
| 1952 | The Dictionary of Mind, Matter and Morals (ed. L. Denonn) |
| 1953 | *The Good Citizen's Alphabet* |
| 1953 | *Satan in the Suburbs* (available from Spokesman) |
| 1954 | *Nightmares of Eminent Persons* (available from Spokesman) |
| 1954 | *Human Society in Ethics and Politics* |
| 1956 | *Logic and Knowledge* (ed. R.C. Marsh) |
| 1956 | *Portraits from Memory* (available from Spokesman) |
| 1957 | *Understanding History* |
| 1957 | *Why I am not a Christian* (ed. P. Edwards) |
| 1958 | *Vital Letters of Russell, Khrushchev, Dulles* |
| 1958 | *Betrand Russell's Best* (ed. R. Egner) |
| 1959 | *Common Sense and Nuclear Warfare* |
| 1959 | *My Philosophical Development* |
| 1959 | *Wisdom of the West* (ed. P. Foulkes) |
| 1960 | *Bertrand Russell Speaks his Mind* |
| 1961 | *Fact and Fiction* |
| 1961 | *Has Man a Future?* |
| 1961 | *The Basic Writing of Bertrand Russell* (ed. R. Egner & L. Denonn) |
| 1963 | *Unarmed Victory* |
| 1965 | *On the Philosophy of Science* (ed. C. Fritz) |
| 1967 | *War Crimes in Vietnam* |
| 1967 | *Autobiography Vol.I Vol. II* 1968, *Vol.III* 1969 |
| 1968 | *The Art of Philosophising* |
| 1969 | *Dear Bertrand Russell* (ed. B. Feinberg & R. Kasrils) |
| 1972 | *The Collected Stories of Bertrand Russell* (ed. B. Feinberg) |
| 1975 | *Mortals and Others* (ed. H. Ruja) |
| 1983 | *The Collected Papers of Bertrand Russell* Vol.1 |
| 1984 | *The Collected Papers of Bertrand Russell* Vol.7 |
| 1984 | *Theory of Knowledge: The 1913 Manuscript* |
| 1985 | *The Collected Papers of Bertrand Russell Vol.12* |
| 1986 | *The Collected Papers of Bertrand Russell Vol.8* |
| 1987 | *The Collected Papers of Bertrand Russell Vol.9* |
| 1988 | *The Collected Papers of Bertrand Russell Vol.13* |
| 1990 | *The Collected Papers of Bertrand Russell Vol.2* |
| 1992 | *The Collected Papers of Bertrand Russell Vol.6* |
| 1992 | *The Selected Letters of Bertrand Russell Vol.1* (ed. N. Griffin) |
| 1993 | *The Collected Papers of Bertrand Russell Vol.3* |
| 1994 | *The Collected Papers of Bertrand Russell Vol.4* |
| 1995 | *Bibliography of Bertrand Russell* (by K. Blackwell & H. Ruja) |
| 1995 | *The Collected Papers of Bertrand Russell Vol.14* |
| 1997 | *The Collected Papers of Bertrand Russell Vol.10* |
| 1997 | *The Collected Papers of Bertrand Russell Vol.11* |
| 2000 | *The Collected Papers of Bertrand Russell Vol.15* |